GREAT MYSTERIES
Relativity
OPPOSING VIEWPOINTS®

Look for these and other exciting *Great Mysteries: Opposing Viewpoints* books:

Alternative Healing by Gail Stewart
Amelia Earhart by Jane Leder
Anastasia, Czarina or Fake? by Leslie McGuire
Animal Communication by Jacci Cole
Artificial Intelligence by Erik Belgum
The Assassination of President Kennedy by Jeffrey Waggoner
Atlantis by Wendy Stein
The Beginning of Language by Clarice Swisher
The Bermuda Triangle by Norma Gaffron
Bigfoot by Norma Gaffron
Custer's Last Stand by Deborah Bachrach
Dinosaurs by Peter & Connie Roop
The Discovery of America by Renardo Barden
El Dorado, City of Gold by Norma Gaffron
ESP by Michael Arvey
Evolution by Marilyn Bailey
Jack the Ripper by Katie Colby-Newton
Life After Death by Tom Schouweiler
Living in Space by Neal Bernards
The Loch Ness Monster by Robert San Souci
Miracles by Michael Arvey
Noah's Ark by Patricia Kite
Pearl Harbor by Deborah Bachrach
Poltergeists by Peter & Connie Roop
President Truman and the Atomic Bomb by Michael O'Neal
Pyramids by Barbara Mitchell
Reincarnation by Michael Arvey
Relativity by Clarice Swisher
The Shroud of Turin by Daniel C. Scavone
The Solar System by Peter & Connie Roop
Stonehenge by Peter & Connie Roop
The Trojan War by Gail Stewart
UFOs by Michael Arvey
Unicorns by Norma Gaffron
Vampires by Daniel C. Scavone
Witches by Bryna Stevens

GREAT MYSTERIES

Relativity

OPPOSING VIEWPOINTS®

by Clarice Swisher

Greenhaven Press, Inc.   P.O. Box 289009, San Diego, California 92128-9009

No part of this book may be reproduced or used in any form or by any means, electronic, mechanical, or otherwise, including but not limited to photocopy, recording, or any information storage and retrieval system, without prior written permission from the publisher.

Library of Congress Cataloging-in-Publication Data

Swisher, Clarice, 1933-
    Relativity : opposing viewpoints / by Clarice Swisher.
      p. cm. — (Great mysteries)
    Includes bibliographical references and index.
    Summary: Explores Einstein's theory of relativity, its initial reception as well as current scientific acceptance of his ideas about time and space, and the mysterious workings of our universe.
    ISBN 0-89908-076-6
    1. Relativity (Physics)—Juvenile literature. 2. Cosmology—Juvenile literature. [1. Relativity (Physics) 2. Cosmology. 3. Einstein, Albert, 1879-1955.]   I. Title. II. Series: Great mysteries (Saint Paul, Minn.)
QC173.575.S93   1990
531.1'1—dc20   90-3910
                                                             CIP
                                                             AC

Every effort has been made to contact owners of copyright material.
© Copyright 1990 by Greenhaven Press, Inc.

For Karin

Contents

	Introduction	7
One	The Search for Order in the Universe	8
Two	The Early Theories	24
Three	Einstein: Ideas About Order Change Forever	46
Four	The Building Blocks	72
Five	The Beginning and the End	92
Six	The Search Goes On	114
	Books for Further Exploration	118
	Additional Sources Consulted	120
	Glossary	122
	Index	125
	Acknowledgments	126
	Picture Credits	127
	About the Author	128

Introduction

This book is written for the curious—those who want to explore the mysteries that are everywhere. To be human is to be constantly surrounded by wonderment. How do birds fly? Are ghosts real? Can animals and people communicate? Was King Arthur a real person or a myth? Why did Amelia Earhart disappear? Did history really happen the way we think it did? Where did the world come from? Where is it going?

Great Mysteries: Opposing Viewpoints books are intended to offer the reader an opportunity to explore some of the many mysteries that both trouble and intrigue us. For the span of each book, we want the reader to feel that he or she is a scientist investigating the extinction of the dinosaurs, an archaeologist searching for clues to the origin of the great Egyptian pyramids, a psychic detective testing the existence of ESP.

One thing all mysteries have in common is that there is no ready answer. Often there are *many* answers but none on which even the majority of authorities agrees. *Great Mysteries: Opposing Viewpoints* books introduce the intriguing views of the experts, allowing the reader to participate in their explorations, their theories, and their disagreements as they try to explain the mysteries of our world.

But most readers won't want to stop here. These *Great Mysteries: Opposing Viewpoints* aim to stimulate the reader's curiosity. Although truth is often impossible to discover, the search is fascinating. It is up to the reader to examine the evidence, to decide whether the answer is there—or to explore further.

"Penetrating so many secrets, we cease to believe in the unknowable. But there it sits nevertheless, calmly licking its chops."

H.L. Mencken, American essayist

One

The Search for Order in the Universe

Since humans first could observe and think and imagine, they have searched for a "design" in their universe. They have searched for a pattern in the way events occur, both in their personal lives and in nature. They have believed that if they could discover the universal design, they could control events and bring order to their lives. Order provides comfort and power and security.

From prehistoric times, the desire to know how the universe works has led humans to develop rituals, stories, theories, and explanations. People during each era have woven these expressions together; the result is their particular design, their answers, about the great mystery of the universe. Since prehistory, there have been many designs. Each design depended on the amount of knowledge available at the time. As new knowledge became available, a new design emerged, opposing the old design but keeping what was still thought to be true from the old. Each new design expanded the perception of time and space. Each new design described a more complex universe. Over the centuries, the design of the universe has proved to be a mystery not yet solved.

In the earliest times, priests and poets sought answers to the mystery. Then scientists and

Opposite: Since humans first began to observe and reason, they have searched for a design in their universe.

Stephen Hawking, British physicist, has devoted his career to finding the universe's design.

philosophers took up the task of finding answers. In recent centuries, scientists and mathematicians have searched for laws that govern the universe.

Stephen Hawking, a British physicist, said in his 1988 book *A Brief History of Time:*

> Ever since the dawn of civilization, people have not been content to see events as unconnected and inexplicable [not able to be explained]. They have craved an understanding of the underlying order of the world. Today we still yearn to know why we are here and where we come from.

Relativity: A New Understanding

During the early years of the twentieth century, a new understanding of the order of the world emerged. This new understanding is called *relativity*. Originated by Albert Einstein, a physicist from Switzerland, the idea of relativity as the underlying design or framework is a new way of thinking about the universe. Relativity means that one occurrence cannot be measured by itself; rather, each occurrence or value or quality is dependent on another. For example, the warmth of a summer day cannot be measured by itself; its warmth is expressed relative to another summer day which may be warmer or colder. Seeing objects relative to other objects was in Einstein's day a new way of seeing or thinking.

In 1905 and 1916, Albert Einstein published important papers explaining new theories based on the idea of relativity. Einstein's theories are not about everyday events in our everyday world. They are about objects in distant space and about the tiny universe of the atom. His theories are about motion, speed, and mass (the substance of an object), and about time and space and matter (what objects are made of). He explained his ideas in terms of relativity, how elements are dependent on one another. In addition, he published mathematical formulas for measuring one thing relative to another.

Relativity is, in many ways, a mystery in itself. In other ways it is an answer to a bigger mystery. It is a new design replacing a previously held design, which replaced a design believed true before that. What concepts have humans developed to explain the universe? What have been the underlying ideas that led to the twentieth-century idea of relativity?

In the earliest stage, magic was the underlying idea to explain the universe. Later, symbolic heroes and supernatural beings gave a sense of order. Next, early people developed scientific explanations for the sun, the stars, and the seasons. Gradually, a design developed that placed the earth at the center of the universe. That concept was opposed when scientists discovered that the sun is at the center of the solar system. Then came relativity. Since Einstein introduced his theories, scientists have been able to explore the nucleus of the atom and the reaches of outer space. Their explorations have led to new ideas about the beginning of the universe and its possible future. Each of these stages developed as views opposing current beliefs; each stage combines new ideas and discoveries with some ideas from the past.

Defining Terms

Before reviewing the ideas that came before relativity, we need to clarify the terms in this search and how the words are used in the discussion. What do we mean by "the universe," "nature," "order," and "design"? And how important is it to see order in the universe?

First, in the search for the underlying design, *universe* means the space a person dwells in, not the universe of stars and planets. In can be a small space that present attention focuses on; it can be a space as big as the mind can imagine. Sometimes when we are busy, our universe extends no farther than our families, our school, our jobs, and our community. At other times, our imagination takes us into the solar system of the planet earth, its moon and sun, and the stars that extend beyond it. In studies of the atom, the mind travels to a universe so tiny it is invisible and can be seen only in the imagination.

Next, what is "nature"? In most people's minds, *nature* means the outdoor world of trees and plants, mountains and plains, and the seas and deserts. But nature has another meaning that has to do with the

"Long ago, to man's naked primitive eye, it seemed simple: He was the pivot around which the universe wheeled."

David Bergamini, *The Universe*

"Interestingly enough, application of the scientific method...has demonstrated that we living creatures inhabit no very special place in the Universe at all."

Eric Chaisson, *Relatively Speaking*

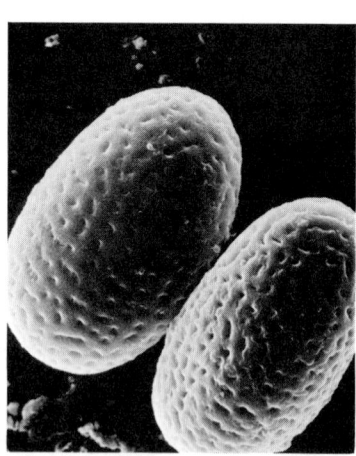

The word *universe* can mean many different things, from the entire cosmos to one person's particular environment to the invisible, microscopic world. Above are shown three universes: Left: A spiral galaxy in the constellation Leo. Center: A boy fishing with his spear in the Amazon River. Right: Fungus spore magnified with an electron microscope.

way things are. For example, it is the nature of dogs to wag their tails when their owners come home; that is the way dogs are. It is the nature of water to flow downhill; that is the way water is. It is the nature of thunder to follow lightning; that is the way electrical storms are. It is the nature of the earth to revolve around the sun; that is the way this solar system works. The word *nature*, in this context, means the way things are.

Order means that events occur repeatedly and dependably. For example, the sun will rise every day; summer will follow spring every year; and a pumpkin seed will produce a pumpkin plant when it is planted in a sunny location and watered. These things happen over and over, and we can expect that they will continue. When we can explain the order of events, we have a *design*.

Our language reflects the value we place on order and the discomfort we associate with disorder. A book of synonyms, a thesaurus, shows that many words for order have a positive tone. One thesaurus lists, for example: "regularity," "normality," "harmony," "tidy," and "ship-shape." It lists a greater number of negative words for disorder: "chance," "chaos," "bungled," "hap-hazard," and "disarray." Most teenagers find that parents approve of neat, orderly rooms with everything in its place; seldom do parents praise a mess. The longing for order is broad and deep.

The Magic Universe

What are some of the earliest views of the universe's design? At the dawn of civilization, primitive people had no philosophers or scientists to explain the world's order. Those early people, like us, observed clues and experienced events. Then they performed rituals. Their rituals implied an order they had no language to explain. They believed their ceremonies helped them control their world, rid it of danger, and bring about good.

George Frazer, a British anthropologist of the late 1800s, studied primitive ceremonies and rituals throughout the world. Frazer studied remnants of the earliest primitive cultures as well as cultures that still practice primitive ways today. From the mass of data he collected, he concluded that early people attempted to explain the design of the universe through laws of magic. Frazer found that similar rituals occurred in many places where people were not likely to have contact with other peoples. He did not believe that one culture taught their rituals to another culture. Rather, he concluded that because people all over the world had the same basic wants, they performed the same rituals based on the same principles.

The Law of Similarity

In his book, *The Golden Bough*, Frazer stated that primitive magic is based on two principles, the *law of*

Everything has its own nature, or "design." It is in the nature, the makeup or design, of a dog to wag its tail.

People search for order because it seems to make their universe easier to understand. Most people prefer order to chaos for this reason. But people's ideas of what is order and what is chaos differ.

similarity and the *law of contagion*. To the people who believed in them, these laws seemed to explain most events in their universe. The law of similarity is that like produces like; performing a miniature event will cause a similar real or bigger event. The law of similarity is also called *homeopathic magic*, from the Greek *homo*, meaning "the same," and *path* meaning "feeling." Through this magic practice, people believed, they could injure or destroy their enemies. For example, an Ojibway Indian made a wooden image of his enemy and then ran a needle into its head or heart while he chanted special sounds. This event supposedly caused the live enemy to feel pain in his head or heart. A primitive Ainu, a member of the earliest known Japanese tribe, made a likeness of a person she wished dead. She buried the likeness head down in a hole under a rotting tree trunk. She then prayed that the person rot with the tree.

Besides injuring or destroying an enemy, the law of similarity, or homeopathic magic, was also used to bring good and keep away bad. For example, in several cultures an image of a baby was thought to bring a child to a couple; binding two images united a couple in love. Furthermore, homeopathic magic worked over long distances and over long time periods. In primitive hunting cultures, wives who spread sleeping mats on the ground and kept a fire burning all night gave their absent husbands comfort and warmth while they were away hunting. A woman in one agricultural society wound many cloths around her head when she planted cabbage seeds, to ensure that full, leafy cabbage heads grew. To bring rain, a man in one farming culture crawled into a tree with a bucket of water, another knocked firesticks together to make lightning, another beat on a pan to make thunder, and another sprinkled water from the bucket onto plants.

The laws of similarity were thought to govern the sun. In Australia, throwing sand into the air and blowing at the same time hurried the sun across the sky and made it set faster beneath the sand where the people thought the sun stayed at night. Egyptians performed a magic ceremony for their sun god Ra. At night when

Sir James Frazer, noted scientist and author of *The Golden Bough*.

Ra went down into darkness, he had to fight with the demons and their leader Apepi. The demons tried to weaken Ra; if Ra were weak, the demons could send clouds out the next day to cover the sun. The Egyptians made a model of the demon leader Apepi in the image of an ugly crocodile or coiled serpent, wrapped the image in papyrus, and tied it with black hair. Then the priest spat on it and stepped on it. The ceremony was supposed to weaken the demons by harming the demon leader. In all of these rituals, people tried to cause an event by performing a smaller event of a similar kind, and magic was the power that made it happen.

The Law of Contagion

The other principle of magic, the law of contagion, assumed that once things had been in contact, they could ever afterwards act on each other. According to this law, a man's footprint could later harm him; an enemy who drove a nail into it could make him lame. By the same law of contagion, primitive people thought blood carried the qualities of the person or animal that it came from. In a hunting culture, drinking or touching an ox's blood made one strong; a lion's blood made one fierce. The hunter and the warrior needed these qualities.

Can an image of a baby cause a family to have a baby? People of some cultures believe so.

The ancient Egyptians were one of several cultures for whom the sun was of supreme importance. They believed that by following magical rituals they could affect the sun's progress.

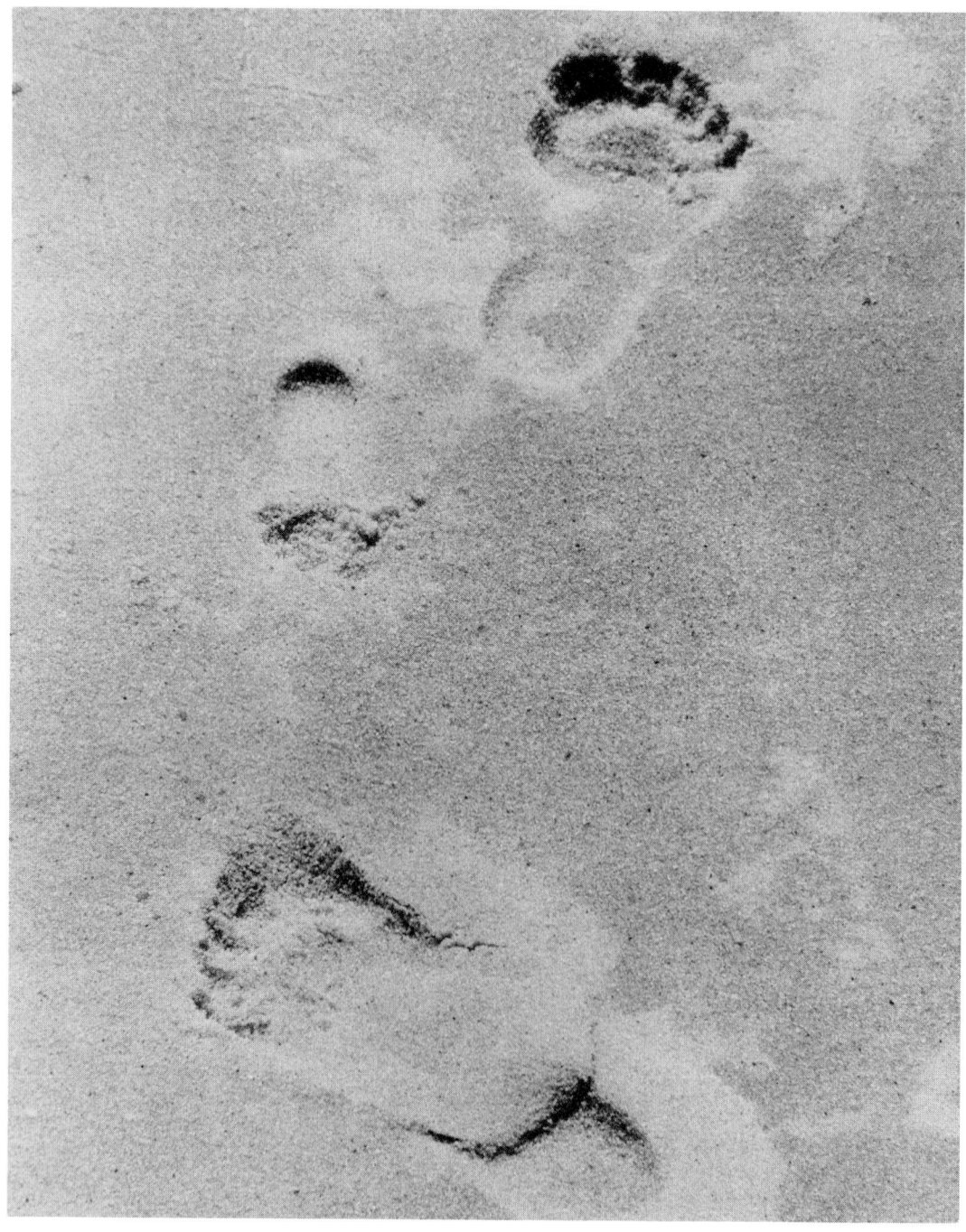

Many cultures have believed that an individual could cause good or harm to come to someone through the laws of similarity and contagion. Some believed, for example, that a person could be harmed by damaging his or her footprints.

In all of these examples, magic was a power that mysteriously crossed space and time. To us it is a mystery how its power could move from object to object and object to person. This design—magic—was a primitive form of relativity in which a big event depended on a small event. As long as people believed it to be true, they practiced the rituals to make the power of magic work.

Since primitive people had no written body of knowledge to draw from, no techniques to do research, and no rules of logic, they ordered their world in the best way they could. Tribes practiced these rituals for many generations. But what happened when the people realized that like failed to produce like, that harming a footprint really did not make a person lame? In many tribes, many years passed while people stubbornly tried to make their familiar order work. Gradually practices died out as people tried new ways to solve the mystery of the order of the universe. Over time, new ways of seeing the world replaced the old.

Heroes and Monsters

In the next stage of development, people told stories that relied on heroes and invisible supernatural beings to protect the people, to bring good, and to avoid bad. Different cultures told their stories for generations; eventually someone wrote down many of them.

While there are many stories from many places, all have a common element—symbols. A hero or a supernatural being symbolized, or represented, order and good; a monster or an evil supernatural power symbolized disorder and destruction. For the psychological security of the storyteller's audience, the hero succeeded and order prevailed. The *Odyssey*, from sixth century B.C. Greece, and *Beowulf*, from seventh century A.D. England, are two stories that illustrate this pattern.

The *Odyssey* is a well-known epic, or story, about a hero that the Greek poet Homer wrote down after the Greeks had told it aloud for generations. The *Odyssey* uses symbols to show the world order. Odysseus, who is a human hero, goes through many difficult adven-

"Our way of thinking in the West sees God as the final source or cause of the energies and wonders of the universe."

Twentieth-century mythologist Joseph Campbell

"If there's a God out there, he's pretty far removed. He set these laws [of the universe] going, and disappeared from sight."

Cosmologist Marc Davis, University of California, Berkeley

Ulysses and his men escaped the Cyclops when Ulysses blinded him. Such stories helped their audience make sense of their world.

tures, but he overcomes his difficulties every time. He symbolizes the way order brings about good. The story also contains invisible supernatural beings; they symbolize the power to make order. Sometimes they cause problems for Odysseus, and sometimes they help him. Monsters and other strange and powerful beings represent danger and destruction. Odysseus overcomes them and right order is restored.

The universe implied in the *Odyssey* extends over a part of the Mediterranean, geographically a small universe. Supernatural beings called gods control the events. Humans, represented by Odysseus, succeed in this universe with wit, courage, and help from the gods. Trouble and danger are part of the order, symbolized by monsters and other strange and powerful beings. Though the hero has temporary struggles, he succeeds in the end. Good wins in this universe of heroes and gods.

Beowulf is also a well-known epic, the first story written in English. The story originated with the early people of Scandinavia, whose descendants told it in England after they invaded and settled there. Beowulf is a hero like Odysseus, and his world also contains monsters and adventures.

Beowulf was a Geat, a member of a tribe living in what is now southern Sweden. He heard about a monster named Grendel who, each night, killed the warriors who served Hrothgar, a Danish king. Beowulf, determined to help, gathered his fourteen best warriors and sailed to the Danish kingdom. There he defeated Grendel by pulling off the monster's arm.

Beowulf eventually became king of the Geats and reigned for fifty years. During that time he fought numerous battles with monsters, slaying them every time, making the northern world safer and more orderly.

In telling and retelling these stories over hundreds of years, the Greeks and the English established a belief in a similar universe. Both groups believed their universe had danger and trouble; both believed humans could bring order to it with strength, wit, courage, and help from heroes or from good supernatural beings. As with magic, the worldview implied in these epics was gradually modified and eventually replaced.

Bible Stories

Stories from the Old Testament in the Bible, some of them told before 500 B.C., best reveal the changes made in the symbolic world of heroes and monsters. First, the universe became bigger, both in space and time. Second, instead of many supernatural beings, good was concentrated in one good God. Instead of a variety of monsters, trouble and evil were concentrated in a single being, the devil or Satan.

The creation story from the book of Genesis best reveals the vision of a greater universe. At the beginning, state the authors of Genesis, chaos, a formless void, filled the entire universe. Then God made order out of this vast chaos, a task which took him six days. He made light and dark; sky, sea, and land; plants and trees; night and day; the four seasons; the sun, the moon, and the stars; fish, fowl, animals, and

In *Beowulf,* the monster Grendel destroyed a king's warriors. But Beowulf, a noble hero, destroyed the monster and restored order to the world.

Among other difficult trials, God afflicted Job with boils. Job's story and others from the Bible showed how God was in charge of the order of the universe.

humans—Adam and Eve. The eighth Psalm emphasizes the vastness of the universe God made and the smallness of the humans in it. The Psalmist says, "When I consider thy heavens, and the work of thy fingers, the moon and the stars, which thou hast ordained; What is man?"

The Old Testament books imply as well that the storytellers envisioned a larger concept of time than primitive peoples had ever imagined. In Psalm 90, the poet tells the listener how long God has existed, compared to a single person's time in the universe. The poet says, "Before the mountains were brought forth, or ever thou hadst formed the earth and the world, even from everlasting to everlasting, thou art God." The poet goes on to compare God's time to a human day: "For a thousand years in thy sight are but as yesterday when it is past, and as a watch in the night." He explains the relatively short length of a human life by saying, "In the morning it flourisheth, and groweth up; in the evening it is cut down and withereth." An important point to note about Psalm 90 is that the poet apparently understands the relativity of time. Time viewed from God's angle is long; time viewed from the human angle is short. To the Psalmist, time is not a fixed entity; neither was it to Einstein.

The story of Job, a story told for thousands of years before it was recorded in the Old Testament, illustrates both the common elements and the changes in the symbolic order of heroes and monsters. Satan, symbolizing the power of darkness and trouble, challenges the power of God, and they agree to a contest. To test who is stronger, they choose Job, a human hero, a good man and one of God's chosen people. Satan thinks he can turn Job away from God and goodness if he brings Job enough trouble.

Satan destroys Job's property and children, covers his body with boils, and turns his wife and his friends against him. Throughout the troubles, Job endures, and he remains true to God. He calls to God to let him die and be relieved of the awful suffering. Finally, God speaks to Job "out of the whirlwind" and reminds Job that he is small and God is great. God speaks to Job in

"Order is Heav'n's first law."

Seventeenth-century English poet and essayist Alexander Pope

"Nothing is orderly till man takes hold of it. Everything in creation lies around loose."

Nineteenth-century American clergyman Henry Ward Beecher

People today still believe in the laws of similarity and contagion. Superstitions such as fearing bad luck if one walks under a ladder are proof of this.

questions that reveal the biblical concept of vast time and space in the universe. God asks Job where Job was when "I laid the foundations of the earth" and "when the morning stars sang together." God reminds Job that he "shut up the sea," "entered the springs of the sea," opened "the gates of death," and "parted" the light. He asks Job if Job had "perceived the breadth of the earth," if he could "send lightnings." After God speaks to Job, he stops the contest, having defeated Satan, and restores Job's possessions and children and grants Job a long and fruitful life.

The tellers of Job's story reveal their awareness of a grand and ordered universe. God's questions imply a long-standing, large, ordered space. Like the world of Odysseus and Beowulf, Job's world has destruction and trouble, but humans prevail with God's help and with the strength of their own character—in Job's case, endurance and commitment. In this view of the universe, order results from the power of a good God and the loyalty and obedience of good people to that God.

What happened to magic and ritual and to belief in heroes and supernatural beings? Are those ways of ordering the universe dead or forgotten? No. These answers to the mystery of the design of the universe still exist in the lives of many individuals today. Today people carry a rabbit's foot for good luck and use caution on Friday the thirteenth to prevent bad luck, but they do so without the serious belief in the power of magic held by primitive people. In personal crises many people still endure as Job did and still call on a god for relief in an effort to find order for their personal lives.

New Knowledge Leads to New Views

Designs based on magic and on symbolic heroes and supernatural powers were designs expressed by the priests and the poets. These designs describe order for the personal worlds people lived in when they had little knowledge about the physical nature of the universe. Eventually the search turned to the mystery of the sun and the stars, the mystery of the physical universe.

Two

The Early Theories

Einstein's twentieth-century theory of relativity is about the physical universe and how to measure things in it. Einstein's theories explain things like motion, energy, time, and space. But Einstein was not the first to try to explain these elements of the universe. The road to relativity is a long one, marked by many earlier theories that have since been rejected or expanded. The theories that turned out to be true helped form the basis of some of Einstein's ideas.

Who developed these earlier theories? The earliest designs were developed by religious leaders and poets. Others were discovered by scientists, mathematicians, and philosophers. These two groups often disagreed with one another over the truth of each other's theories, though occasionally they did work together. For both groups, finding answers to the mystery of the universe involved observation, reason, and imagination.

Imagine living thousands of years ago and trying to figure out the physical universe for the first time. The ancient people had to start with basic questions: What is the sun and why does it rise and set? What are the stars? Why do seasons change? What is the earth and does it move or stand still? Why are there day and night? What is light? How big is the universe? Does it

Opposite: Imagine being a person from thousands of years ago, without our advantage of centuries of recorded knowledge, trying to figure out how the universe works.

Early people tried to solve the mysteries of the seasons. They began to see patterns in nature, such as the crocus (above) being a sign that the season was beginning to change from winter to spring.

have an outer edge? How do planets and stars move and why do they move? What is everything made of? What is time?

The first answers were to questions about the earth's mysteries: the seasons and the form of the earth and sky. Then discoveries were made that placed the earth at the center of the universal order. Gradually, a sun-centered design replaced the earth-centered design. How did these discoveries come about? Who contributed knowledge and ideas? How did the discoverers find answers?

Early Ideas

The earliest discoverers, whose names are unknown, tried to solve the mystery of the seasons. We assume they wanted to know why days got shorter and weather changed. Perhaps they wanted to know when to plant crops and when to harvest. At one time people thought magic and sacrifices to the gods could control weather and the seasons. Later, they used more scientific methods. They began to figure out accurate ways of marking the position of the sun and the change in the seasons. Evidence of ancient ways to measure time still exists.

The ancient rock arrangement in southwestern England called Stonehenge is an old time-measuring device built around 2500 B.C. It is evidence that its builders had found a pattern, or order, in their universe.

Stonehenge, an ancient stone monument in England, was a primitive calendar.

Stonehenge, which means "hanging stones," consists of several enormous rocks placed to make arches; down the hill from the arches there are two large stones opposite each other. On February 5 and November 8, a person standing in the center of the stone arches can see the sunrise lined up over the stone down the hill and through the center of an arch. On May 6 and August 8, a viewer can see the sunset lined up over the opposite stone and through the center of an opposite arch. These dates occur approximately forty-five days from the spring and fall equinoxes and summer and winter solstices. Equinoxes occur in March and September when day and night have equal length. Solstices occur in June and December when the length of day and night are most unequal. By figuring out the sun's patterns, the people were able to make these great stones a calendar which told them when to plant and when to harvest.

The Great Pyramid at Giza in Egypt also measured the seasons. Although built for another purpose, it was placed so that the sun's shadows accurately measured the seasons' changes.

Besides charting the seasons' changes, ancient people were curious about the shape of the earth and sky. Evidence from several places in the Middle East indicate that early people thought that the earth and sky were flat, like a floor and a ceiling.

Ancient Egyptians thought the sky was a canopy held up by mountains at the four corners of the earth, something like a canopied four-poster bed. Astronomers climbed stairs and hills to be closer to the stars. On the hilltops they made rough measurements of the location of stars. They used measurements taken from rocks, wooden quadrants (instruments for measuring), or their crossed fingers. Other people still thought the sun swam at night from west to east in a river beneath the flat earth.

Earth as Center of the Universe

Beginning around the fifth century B.C., Greek philosophers and astronomers developed an earth-centered model of the universe. According to this model, the earth was a stationary sphere, a round ball

"Aristarchus of Samos brought out a book consisting of some hypotheses, in which the premises lead to the result that the universe is many times greater than that now so called. His hypotheses [include] that the fixed stars and the Sun remain unmoved, that the Earth revolves about the Sun..., the Sun lying in the middle of the orbit."

Early Greek mathematician Archimedes

"As an old man, [Plato] 'was very sorry,' reports historian Plutarch, 'that he had located the earth in the center of the universe, in a place not fitting for it... since the central and most noble place should be reserved for something more worthy.'"

David Bergamini, *The Universe*

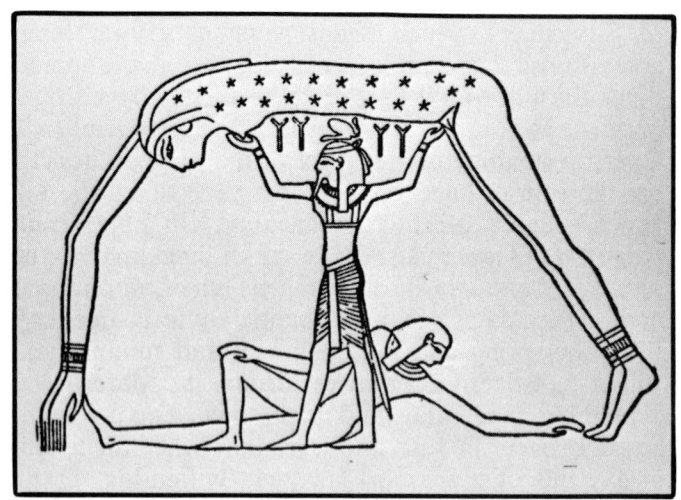

Right: Early Egyptians believed the sky was a canopy hanging over a flat earth. Opposite: This medieval German woodcut shows how most people before Copernicus believed the universe looked. Note that the earth (*terra*) is at the center.

at the center of the universe, and the planets and stars moved on crystal spheres nestled within other crystal spheres. The planets moved in complicated motions on the inner spheres, and the stars moved in fixed positions on the outer spheres. All moved through *aether*, a gel-like clear substance that filled all the spaces between spheres.

This design of the universe was a three-dimensional model, with length, width, and height. It gradually replaced the flat-earth model, which had only length and width. (Much later Einstein introduced a fourth dimension to the design.) This earth-centered model was considered the "true" design from around 500 B.C. until A.D. 1600.

Four scholars, Plato, Eudoxus, Aristotle, and Ptolemy, were especially important in developing this design. They agreed on the earth-centered concept but viewed the details differently.

Plato, who lived from 427 to 347 B.C., was a Greek philosopher and educator. In 387 B.C., he founded an academy outside the city of Athens for the study of philosophy and science. Plato admired perfect geometric forms, especially the circle. He described his vision of the universe in the last chapter of his book, *The Republic*. He envisioned the universe in perfect spheres, as a beautiful and harmonious system of motion and sound in which planets moved and sirens

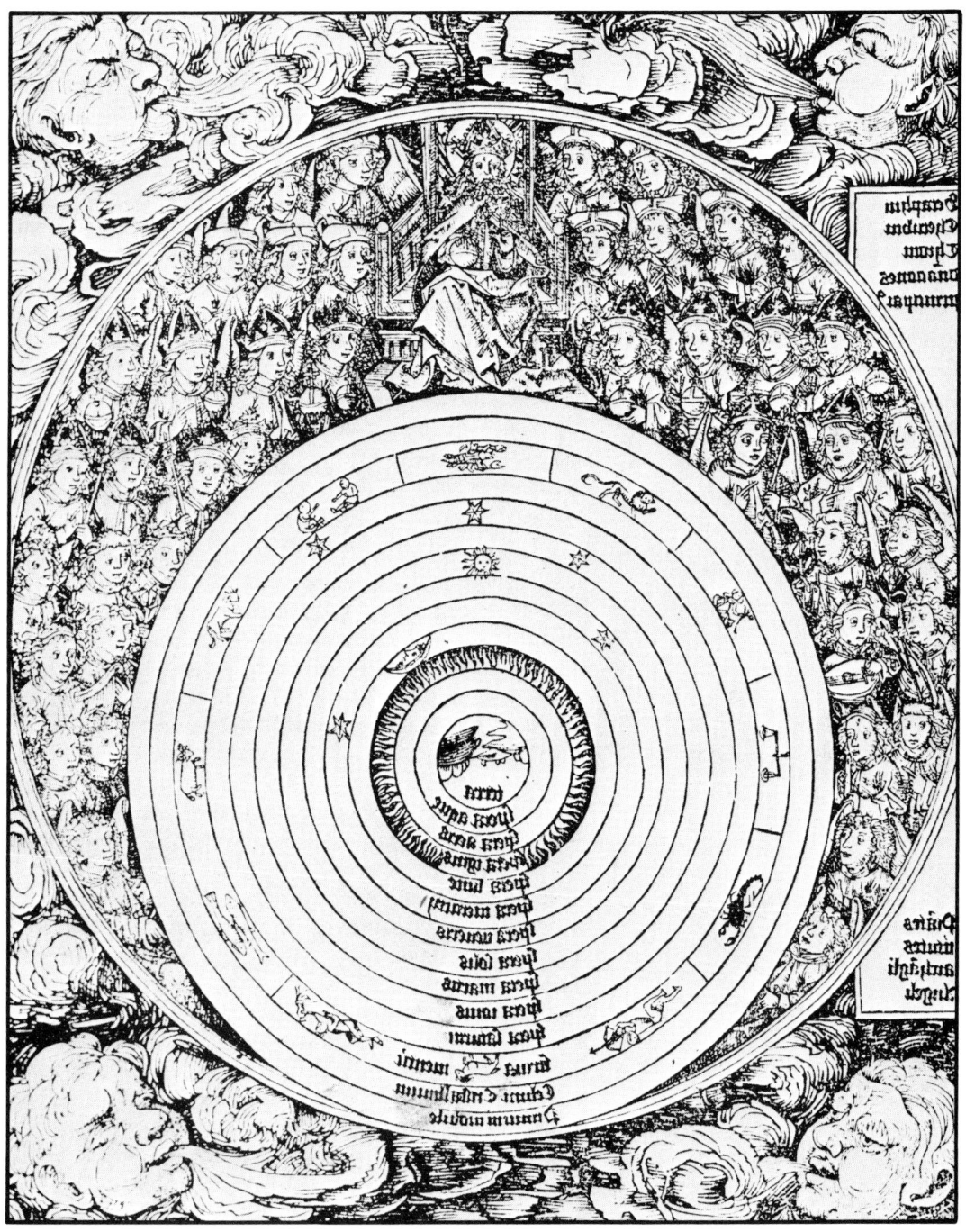

> "[The stars] are at an immense height away.... How exceedingly vast is the godlike work of the Best and Greatest Artist."
>
> Nicolaus Copernicus, founder of modern astronomy

> "[Copernicus is] an upstart astrologer.... This fool wishes to reverse the entire science of astronomy [by saying the sun stands still and the earth moves around it]."
>
> Theologian Martin Luther

sang. (In mythology, siren songs were beautiful musical sounds calling sailors.) He wrote in *The Republic*, "One sound, one note, and from all eight [planets] there was a concord of single harmony."

Eudoxus, another Greek philosopher, studied for a time at Plato's academy and then studied on his own. He mapped the sky from the observatory he built on the bank of the Nile River in Egypt. He agreed with Plato that the earth was at the center of the universe, but he disagreed on two points. Instead of eight planets, Eudoxus identified twenty-seven spheres surrounding the earth. Instead of harmony, he said the earth "dragged and tugged" at the sun, moon, and planets and changed their paths and their velocities (the speed of their motion).

Aristotle and Ptolemy

Aristotle followed Eudoxus's model, but he made further changes. Aristotle was a Greek philospher who lived from 384 to 322 B.C. He studied at Plato's academy for twenty years. In 340 B.C. he published his ideas in a book called *On the Heavens*. He too said the earth was at the center, but he thought fifty-five spheres surrounded it. Nothing existed beyond them, he said, not even space. Within the spheres, every heavenly body had a natural and proper place. Every body tended to stay in its proper place unless it was pushed or pulled from it. But the earth, at the center, could be neither pushed nor pulled; it was immovable. Something immovable is said to be absolute, having a certain position.

Understanding why and how the celestial bodies and other objects moved was part of the search for order. Aristotle developed theories about motion from his idea about proper places. First, he said there was a natural circular motion, the unending, repeating pattern of planets and stars rotating around the earth. Second, there was violent motion which resulted when the earth pushed or pulled a body out of its proper place. When that happened, the pushed or pulled body, or planet, naturally returned to its proper place. Third, there were straight-up and straight-down motions, the directions bodies took when they returned to

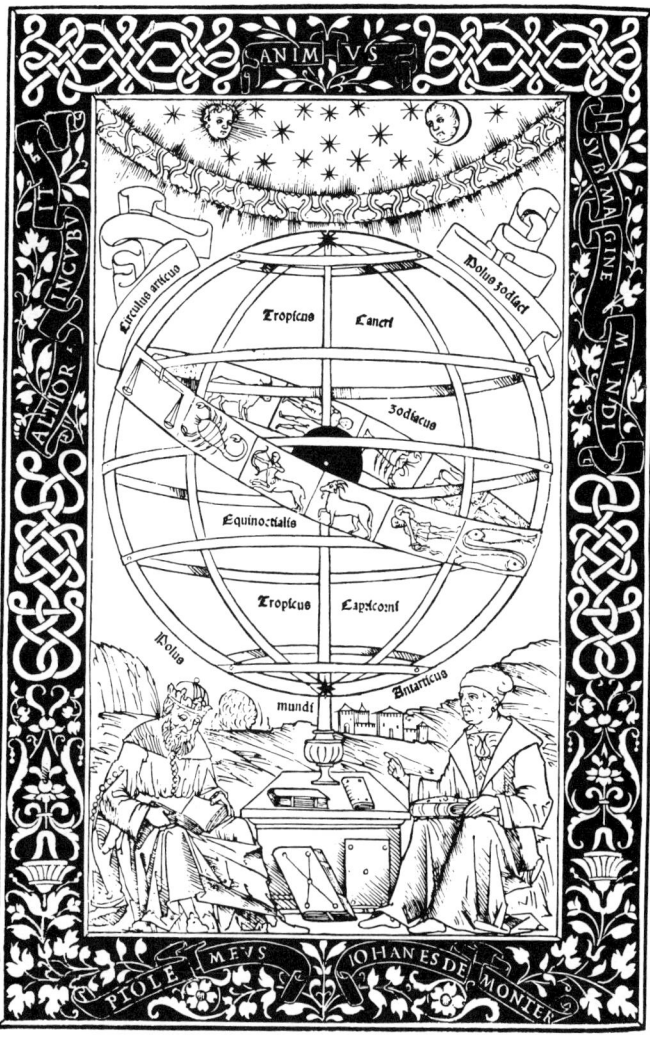

This illustration was made for a 1496 translation of Ptolemy's *Almagest*. The book described Ptolemy's vision of the universe.

their proper places. Aristotle had seen smoke rise and stones fall; he reasoned that planets moved in the same ways. Finally, Aristotle said that a heavy body or object fell straight down faster than a lighter object. Aristotle's laws of motion can be restated this way: A body tends to stay in its natural, proper place unless it is driven by a force or impulse; if it is dislodged by a force, the body returns to its proper place.

Ptolemy, born around 150 A.D., was an Egyptian

philosopher and astronomer. He tried to see where the planets and stars were and how they moved. He studied the sky from an observatory near Alexandria, Egypt, and made charts and tables of what he saw. His charts show eight spheres around the earth: one each for the moon, Mercury, Venus, the sun, Mars, Jupiter, and Saturn, and one for the fixed stars, the stars that stay in the same place all the time. His charts also show, for the first time, satellites (moons) spinning around Jupiter. In addition, Ptolemy made tables showing the location of 1,022 stars in forty-eight constellations, or groups. He determined that the universe measured fifty million miles from the earth to the edge.

Today we know the universe is much, much larger. Ptolemy's whole universe could fit inside the earth's orbit around the sun as we know it. Even though Ptolemy's measurements and charts were wrong, his work was important because he developed methods for studying the universe. He made direct observations; he recorded his findings on charts and tables; and he used numbers to represent locations. These methods were followed by later scientists and mathematicians. Out of a sky filled with millions of dots of light, Ptolemy found order.

These four ancient philosophers and scientists formed theories about the same concepts that Einstein did many centuries later. They formed their answers about the location, distance, and motion of celestial bodies in space. They assumed that the universe was absolute, that it had a fixed design that they could discover. Einstein's theory of relativity opposed this assumption.

Important Questions

These ancient philosophers and scientists seemed to know what questions were most important for solving the mystery of the universe. As Einstein did later, they also developed theories about time, matter, and light. Some of their theories were later proved wrong, but a few are remarkably similar to Einstein's ideas, as we will see later.

Aristotle posed the question: What is time? Aristotle thought time was absolute; that is, a determined

> "[To teach that the sun is the center of the universe would be] a very dangerous attitude and one calculated...to injure our holy faith by contradicting the Scriptures."
>
> Cardinal Robert Ballarmine, Master of Controversial Questions at the Roman College, sixteenth century

> "I do not think it necessary to believe that the same God who gave us our senses, our speech, our intellect, would have us put aside the use of these, to teach us instead such things as with their help we could find out for ourselves, particularly in the case of these sciences, of which there is not the smallest mention in the Scriptures."
>
> Sixteenth-century astronomer and physicist Galileo Galilei

amount of time existed between events no matter who measured it or from what space it was measured. According to Aristotle's view, both time and space were absolute, both fixed and separate from one another. For example, according to Aristotle's idea, the time it takes to play a soccer game would be the same if it could be measured by someone next to the field in Portsmith, Iowa, someone in Sydney, Australia, or someone on the planet Venus. A minute is the same every place on earth and every place in the universe. Neither the space, or place, nor the measurer affected time. Aristotle's idea about absolute time was accepted until the twentieth century when Albert Einstein proposed a different idea.

Another question was: What is matter? Matter is what things are made of. Aristotle, like many others, thought all matter contained only four elements, or ingredients: earth, water, air, and fire. He thought matter could be divided into smaller and smaller bits without limit. On the other hand, Democritus, a Greek philosopher from Plato's time, thought matter was made up of atoms and the empty space between them. He thought that atoms were solid and that they move. In Greek, *atom* means "indivisible," or "cannot be divided." Democritus thought different objects had atoms of different shape, arrangement, and position. He thought atoms came together, collided, rebounded, scattered, and then disappeared. These two different ideas about the nature of matter remained in conflict for many centuries until 1905 when Einstein discovered a way to study the atom.

Finally, the ancient philosophers asked the question: What is light? Plato and Euclid, the inventor of a system of geometry, thought that light was made of streamers that went out from the eyes. Pythagoras, a Greek philosopher and mathematician, thought light was made of tiny particles moving from the lighted bodies to the eyes. Empedocles, another Greek philosopher, thought light was composed of high-speed waves. Streamers, particles, or waves—what was light? The answers of these philosophers were debated until the twentieth century when experiments could settle the issue.

The ancient philosopher Aristotle asked and answered many questions about the nature of the universe.

Plato and Euclid thought that light was made of streamers that traveled out through the eyes. Pythagoras thought it was tiny particles moving from the seen object to the eyes of the person viewing it.

The Dark Ages

From approximately 500 B.C. until A.D. 300, more than eight hundred years, the dominant idea was that the universe was ordered around the earth. But then, in the Western world, the search for answers stopped for more than a thousand years. Around A.D. 400, the Romans and the Christians shut down exploration of the universe, and these Dark Ages, as they were named, lasted until 1500. Attention during the Dark Ages shifted away from the physical universe to the best ways to live a personal life on earth to serve God. How did this shift come about?

St. Augustine was one of many Christian church authorities who opposed study of the universe. St. Augustine, a North African who lived from A.D. 354 to 430, was a brilliant youth sent to study at the finest academies. In 384, when he went to Milan, Italy, to teach, the Catholic bishop converted him to Christianity. Later, St. Augustine wrote *The City of God*, a book defending Christianity and the Catholic Church. In the book he said that God had created the universe, as described in Genesis, around 5000 B.C. By accepting the creation story as fact, little further study was necessary. The design of the universe was clear from the account in Genesis. St. Augustine said that time is the property of the created universe and did not exist before God created it. Thus, St. Augustine had fixed both space and time, and the universe seemed not to be a mystery any longer. St. Augustine and others found the order they sought in religion.

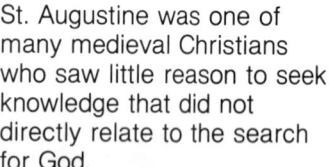

St. Augustine was one of many medieval Christians who saw little reason to seek knowledge that did not directly relate to the search for God.

Another church convert named Tertullian said that curiosity was no longer necessary. St. Ambrose, bishop of Milan, told why; he said that discussing nature and the position of the bodies in the physical universe did nothing to help people in their hope for a life to come. He meant a hope for life after death in heaven. Timothy Ferris, a twentieth-century astronomer, wrote in his book, *Coming of Age in the Milky Way:*

> Conservative churchmen modeled the universe after the tabernacle of Moses; as a tabernacle was a tent, the sky was demoted from a glorious sphere to its prior status as a low tent roof.... The proud round earth was hammered flat; likewise the shimmering sun. Behind the sky reposed eternal Heaven, accessible only through death.

The Renaissance

The search for solutions to the mysteries of the universe and the nature of its design appeared to be dead. And it remained dead for more than a thousand years while people turned to personal matters of life on earth and afterlife in heaven. But human curiosity never dies entirely. The search for order came alive again in an age called the Renaissance. The word *renaissance* means "rebirth." The Renaissance was a reawakening of learning that spread throughout Europe, beginning in the fourteenth century in Italy. During this time all learning thrived: philosophy, music, art, literature, science, and mathematics. During the fifteenth century, scholars again took up the questions the ancient philosophers had asked about the universe. They corrected errors, invented new equipment to observe the stars, and arrived at new answers. They determined that the sun is at the center of the universe and the planets revolve around it. The whole universe, they finally concluded, operated like a machine, held in working order by a force called gravity.

The new solution to the mystery of the universe's design came about in steps. Some philosophers identified procedures to use; other philosophers and mathematicians worked on different parts of the

The Renaissance, a time of rebirth of learning and the seeking of new knowledge about the universe, began in the fifteenth century. Leonardo da Vinci, a brilliant man of numerous scientific and artistic talents, was the symbolic man of the age. This drawing is from his notebooks.

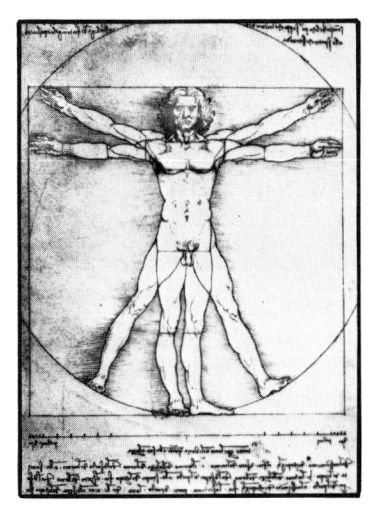

Top: Sir Francis Bacon described the empirical method of reasoning—going from observations and experience to deduction. Bottom: René Descartes believed intuition was the key to understanding.

mystery. Eventually, the pieces fitted together into the new answer.

Scholars from many countries worked on the mystery. Francis Bacon, a philosopher from England, and René Descartes, a philosopher from France, clarified methods of thinking useful for solving scientific mysteries. Nicolaus Copernicus, Tycho Brahe, Johannes Kepler, Galileo Galilei, and Isaac Newton each contributed partial answers; the accumulated answers resulted in the new sun-centered concept. Let us look, now, at the questions that interested these men and the answers they discovered.

At the academy near Athens, Plato and Aristotle had developed theories of knowledge, systematic methods of thinking that were useful for solving problems. Renaissance philosophers rediscovered them and brought them into common use. Francis Bacon described the empirical method, which depends on observation. He said humans gain knowledge by first using their senses—their eyes and ears—to observe nature. After many observations and much experience, one can see patterns emerge and eventually discover nature's laws. Astronomers used Bacon's empirical method, which was earlier practiced by Ptolemy. They observed the sky from observatories and then made tables that showed the location and time of stars' appearances.

René Descartes developed his theory of knowledge by doubting. He doubted every idea he knew until he came to one he could not doubt, the idea that "I think; therefore, I am." Descartes based his theory on reasoning because humans think. Descartes said the human mind acquires ideas intuitively; that is, a whole idea comes into the mind at once. To test the idea's truth and find its usefulness, the person breaks down the intuitive idea into all its parts, studies them, and puts them into logical order. For example, when George Frazer learned that primitive people made images like people and then stuck pins into the images, he must have wondered why they did that. He had an intuitive idea at the moment he figured it out and perhaps said, "I get it; they think sticking the image hurts the person." He could then go on to analyze the parts of the ritual and put them in order, concluding that the people believed like produces like.

The Sun-Centered Universe

Bacon and Descartes brought back the methods used in Plato's academy, and Nicolaus Copernicus reawakened the search for the universe's order. While doing so, he took the earth out of the center and put the sun there instead. Born in Poland in 1473, Copernicus studied and read at the best schools and at libraries and in his own private library. The printing press had been invented just thirty years before his birth, and Copernicus could read thousands of volumes written by the ancient philosophers. He read Plato's, Aristotle's, and Ptolemy's explanations of the earth-centered universe. He also read about Aristarchus, a Greek mathematician from Aristotle's time. Aristarchus had drawn geometrical figures of celestial

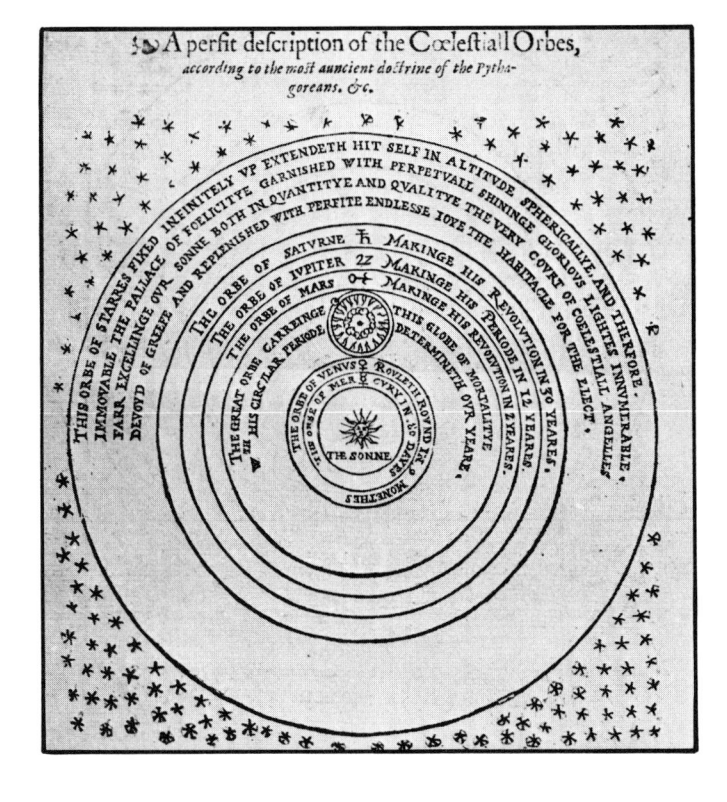

Right: Nicolaus Copernicus. Left: An English adaptation of his view of the solar system. The sun (*sonne*) is at the center.

The astronomer Tycho Brahe spent twenty years making charts of the stars.

bodies that stretched across the sky, and he had calculated that the sun was bigger than the earth. He had thought it made no sense that a big body revolved around a smaller one, and he had concluded that the sun was at the center. But his ideas had received little or no attention at the time he wrote them. Aristotle's and Ptolemy's earth-centered concept had prevailed.

As a result of his studies, Copernicus concluded that the sun is at the center of the solar system and the earth and planets revolve around it. He tried to make more accurate calculations than Ptolemy's, but he could never make them work out any better. The problem was that Copernicus calculated for circular revolutions; today we know the planets make elliptical revolutions. (An elliptical shape is like a circle slightly flattened.) Nonetheless, Copernicus had contributed a partial new theory and refuted an old, wrong one.

Tycho Brahe, a sixteenth-century Danish astronomer, also took up the search for answers where an ancient philosopher had left off. In 1572 Brahe saw a supernova, a violently exploding star; he could see that it was beyond the sun. In 1577 he observed a comet; he knew it was beyond the moon. When he watched an eclipse, he could tell that the sun and the planets were not in the positions the ancient philosophers had said they were. Ptolemy's tables, charting positions of stars and the motion of planets, were wrong. Brahe built an observatory near Copenhagen, Denmark, and equipped it with huge brass quadrants, or measuring instruments, that could make accurate measurements. Brahe worked in his observatory for twenty years and made new, accurate tables charting the positions of stars and rotations of planets. Although Brahe was a skilled observer and an accurate recorder, he was unable to complete his empirical process; he never saw new patterns or discovered new laws. Another scientist, Johannes Kepler, completed Brahe's work.

A German astronomer and mathematician born in 1600, Johannes Kepler was a shy, sickly man whose clothes and behavior made people laugh. Once while lecturing to a class he stopped in the middle of a sentence because an idea about orbiting planets came to him intuitively. He read Plato and Aristotle and loved Plato's description of the unity and harmony of the spheres making music in siren songs. He longed to develop theories for the circular rotations Plato described, but to do so he needed facts about the locations of stars and planets. Brahe had the tables—the data—and Kepler acquired them after Brahe's death.

After many years of trying to develop theories for circular orbits, Kepler realized that planets travel in ellipses, not circles. Kepler also discovered that planets rotate faster through the part of their orbit that is nearer the sun. He was able to calculate a planet's distance from the sun from its orbital time, the time it takes a planet to orbit the sun once. Kepler said, "I contemplate its [the solar system's] beauty with incredible and ravishing delight."

Galileo

Now that Copernicus, Brahe, and Kepler had provided a new solution to the mystery of the design of the universe—a sun-centered planetary system—what remained? Galileo Galilei, an astronomer and physicist born in Pisa, Italy, in 1564, saw three important problems. He saw the need for a better telescope to gather more accurate data, a better understanding of the laws

Left: Johannes Kepler. Right: A page from Kepler's *Epitomes Astronomiae Copernicanea*. Kepler figured out that the planets travel in elliptical, not circular, patterns.

Galileo Galilei continued to work on his theories about the universe even while he was in prison for not conforming to the teachings of his time.

governing motion, and public acceptance of the sun-centered design.

Galileo frequently has received credit for inventing the telescope, but he did not. He improved it, used it, and told what he saw with it. He looked at the moon and saw its rough surface. He looked at Jupiter and saw its four moons, first seen by Ptolemy fourteen hundred years earlier. He looked at Venus and saw its shapes of light and shadow as it revolved around the sun. He looked at the stars. He described what he saw in a book called *The Starry Messenger*, a book that became popular in Italy and as far away as China. It dealt a deathblow to the Aristotle-Ptolemy theory of an earth-centered universe. Galileo wrote, "With absolute necessity we shall conclude...that Venus revolves about the sun as do all the other planets." His book also ended the belief that stars moved on fixed spheres, or orbits, and that nothing, not even space, existed beyond them, as Aristotle had theorized. Galileo wrote about galaxies and said that he saw "innumerable stars grouped together in clusters." He said that some were large and quite bright, "while the number of small ones is quite beyond calculation." What Galileo saw and described expanded the depth of space and opened up the universe.

Galileo's research for *The Starry Messenger* provided the answer to his first problem, the need for more accurate data about the heavens. He then went to work on the second problem, discovering the laws that govern motion. The mystery about motion had two parts: How and why do planets move in orbits instead of straight lines, and why do objects fall to the earth when they are dropped? Aristotle had said that a circular motion was a natural motion, but that did not explain *why*. Aristotle had also said that heavy objects fall faster than light objects. Was he right? Galileo set up experiments to solve the mystery of motion, an important problem in the search for order.

The popular story says that Galileo experimented by dropping objects from the Leaning Tower of Pisa. A more accurate account is that he experimented by rolling lead balls of different weights down smooth, slanted surfaces. The lead balls and slanted surfaces worked better than dropping the balls from the Tower because they moved more slowly, and Galileo could measure more accurately how fast they moved. Galileo made two discoveries from these experiments. First, a heavy lead ball and a lighter lead ball traveled down the slope at the same speed. Second, both balls speeded up, or accelerated, as they traveled. Both of these results are true as long as the air does not interfere by slowing down or speeding up the balls. These experiments partially solved the mystery of how and why objects fall to the earth.

One of Galileo's experiments determined that a small, heavy ball and a large, light ball would fall at the same rate of speed.

> "And Newton, something more than man,
> Div'd into nature's hidden springs,
> Laid bare the principles of things,
> Above the earth our spirits bore,
> And gave us worlds unknown before."
>
> Eighteenth-century poet Charles Churchill

> "Even before man knew of other galaxies or realized the enormous distances with which he had to cope, Newton's beautiful equations had begun to be questioned."
>
> David Bergamini, *The Universe*

Finally, Galileo campaigned to convert the Roman Catholic Church to the Copernican design of the universe. He wanted church authorities to revise interpretation of Scripture to reflect the sun-centered view. But he set out too boldly and offended church authorities. Instead of accepting Galileo's plan, they banned Copernicus's book, *On the Revolutions*, and arrested Galileo. Galileo finally had to renounce his Copernican ideas. He said in court, "I do abjure, damn, and detest the said errors and heresies...[that are] contrary to the Holy Church....I shall never again speak or assert, orally or in writing, such things." An unidentified person reported that when Galileo left the court that day he said, "In spite of what I have been forced to say here, the earth *does* circle the sun." Galileo spent his last years in his home outside Florence, Italy, under house arrest. During those years he studied motion, looked at the sky through his telescope, and wrote another book based on the Copernican model. He smuggled this final work to Holland, where it was published. Galileo died in 1642, without making peace with the Catholic Church.

Newton's Gravity

Isaac Newton, an English mathematician and physicist, found another vital clue to the mystery of the sun-centered universe. He applied the data from Brahe's tables, Kepler's discovery of elliptical rotations, and Galileo's conclusions about falling bodies to the Copernican model. In this way he determined the general laws of motion and the laws of gravity. His laws of gravity applied to everything in the known universe, from a stone on earth to a planet in space.

Newton explained his laws of motion in 1687 in a book known as *Principia*. There are three general laws of motion, he wrote. The first law is that a body, or object, will stay at rest unless some force acts on it. In other words, a bowling ball sitting on a flat box will stay still unless, for example, someone pushes it or someone tilts the box. The first law also says that a body or object moves in a straight line unless some force acts on it to change its direction. The bowling ball rolls in a straight line unless, for example, the floor

Sir Isaac Newton figured out laws of gravity that remained unchallenged until the twentieth century.

is uneven, someone pushes it, or it bounces off another object.

The second law describes what happens once some force has acted on an object. The object will move, but how fast depends on two things: how strong the force is and how much mass the object has. (Mass is the amount of matter in a body, essentially how big and heavy it is.) In other words, a normal-size bowling ball pushed hard will move faster than one pushed lightly. But an over-sized bowling ball will move slower with the same amount of push.

The third law is that for every action there is always an equal reaction; action and reaction make a pair of forces. In other words, if a bowling ball rolls into a person's ankle, the amount of force the bowling ball has when it hits is the same as the amount of force felt on the person's ankle. Those forces are equal; one cannot be a stronger force than the other.

Mysteries of Gravity

After Newton developed these three principles about motion, he used them in developing laws of

Newton found that larger, more massive bodies have stronger gravity fields than smaller, less dense bodies do.

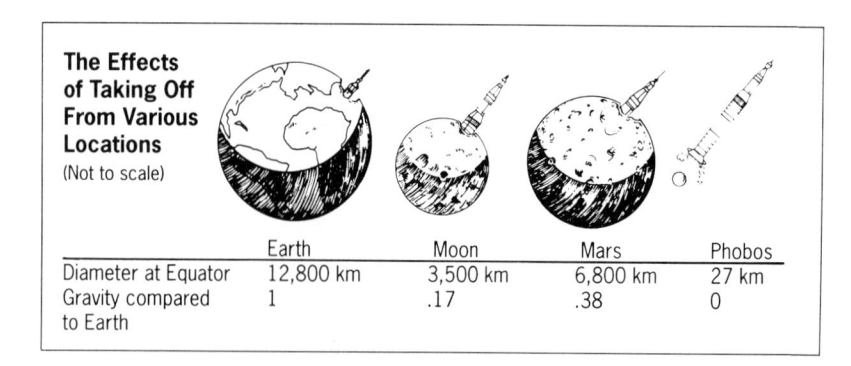

The Effects of Taking Off From Various Locations
(Not to scale)

	Earth	Moon	Mars	Phobos
Diameter at Equator	12,800 km	3,500 km	6,800 km	27 km
Gravity compared to Earth	1	.17	.38	0

gravity. How did Newton figure out what the laws of gravity are? The popular story says that Newton worked by a window, and there was an apple orchard outside the window. When he saw an apple fall, the idea came to him: The force that made an apple fall must be the same force that makes the whole sun-centered universe work! It was an intuitive idea, as Descartes had described. Newton's laws of gravity answer three questions about motion in the physical universe. One, what determines the amount of gravity, or force, a body has? Two, what explains why a heavy and a light object fall in a vacuum (a space without air) at the same rate? And, three, how does distance affect gravity, or force?

Newton found that the amount of gravity, or the amount of attracting force, that a body has is related to its mass. Big planets have more attracting force or gravity than small ones. For example, the earth has greater attracting power than the moon, which is smaller and less dense. On the other hand, the earth has less attracting force or gravity than Jupiter, which is a bigger planet.

In addition, Newton found out why a light and a heavy object fall at the same speed in a vacuum. He discovered that the weight of an object speeds its rate of fall, and its mass slows its rate of fall. He compared a large, light and a small, heavy ball. The heavy ball should drop faster because it is heavier. However, the bigger ball has greater mass and, consequently, a greater resistance to earth's gravity. The smaller ball has less mass and, consequently, drops more slowly. It also has less resistance to the earth's gravity, giving it more downward speed. Thus, the power of weight and the amount of mass resisting the fall equalizes the force for both light and heavy objects, and they fall at the same rate.

Another law of gravity shows the effect of distance. Newton found that the farther apart two bodies are, the weaker is the force between them. He developed a way to calculate the relationship between distance and force. He used two stars to illustrate his point, one twice as far from the earth as the other. The star twice as far away has only one-fourth the gravity or force of the nearer star.

A Clockwork Universe

When Newton established his laws of motion and gravity, he worked out all of the mathematical calculations so that he could predict the motion of all objects. He could predict the motion of a falling rock on earth or a planet orbiting the sun. These laws explain why planets are pulled by force to rotate around the sun instead of flying off in a straight line into space. Newton's laws of motion and gravity seemed to solve the riddle of the sun-centered universe. The universe was predictable and accurate. It worked like a clock that kept running endlessly.

Newton and many people from his time and later assumed that no human could have set the machine-like universe in order, nor could humans keep track of all its moving parts. Therefore, God must have been its maker; the all-knowing mind of God that started it also kept track of its workings. The clockwork universe was accepted as the "true" design from Newton's time until the twentieth century.

Yet scientists continued to doubt, as Descartes had doubted, and continued to think, as Plato had thought, and continued to observe, as Galileo had observed. New questions arose about space and time, matter and motion. Let us look next at the discoveries Albert Einstein made at the beginning of the twentieth century to see how he proved that the Newtonian universe was still only a partial solution to the mystery of the universe's order.

Three

Einstein: Ideas About Order Change Forever

For nearly three centuries, the universe seemed to hum along as Newton had predicted it would. Stars and planets in the heavens and objects on earth behaved according to Newton's laws. The Renaissance had revived the ancient philosophers' questions and had given birth to new answers that seemed, for a long time, to be the right answers. Over time, Newton's laws of motion and gravity came to be thought of as classical, or Newtonian thought, a comfortable way for people to think about their lives in a secure world of absolute space and time. The mystery of order appeared to be solved.

Then, in 1905, a little known man who worked in a Bern, Switzerland, patent office published theories based on a new idea called relativity. The man was Albert Einstein. Relativity opposed Newtonian thought. According to Newtonian thought, the universe is a fixed and certain place—absolute, as we call it. With observation and thought, the absolute universe can be discovered and known by the human mind. Relativity is a different perception about the universe. It says that while the universe may be a fixed and certain place in some ways, its objects constantly change and move. Therefore, we can never know anything accurately because objects change and

Opposite: Albert Einstein, the genius who challenged Newton's idea of a "clockwork universe."

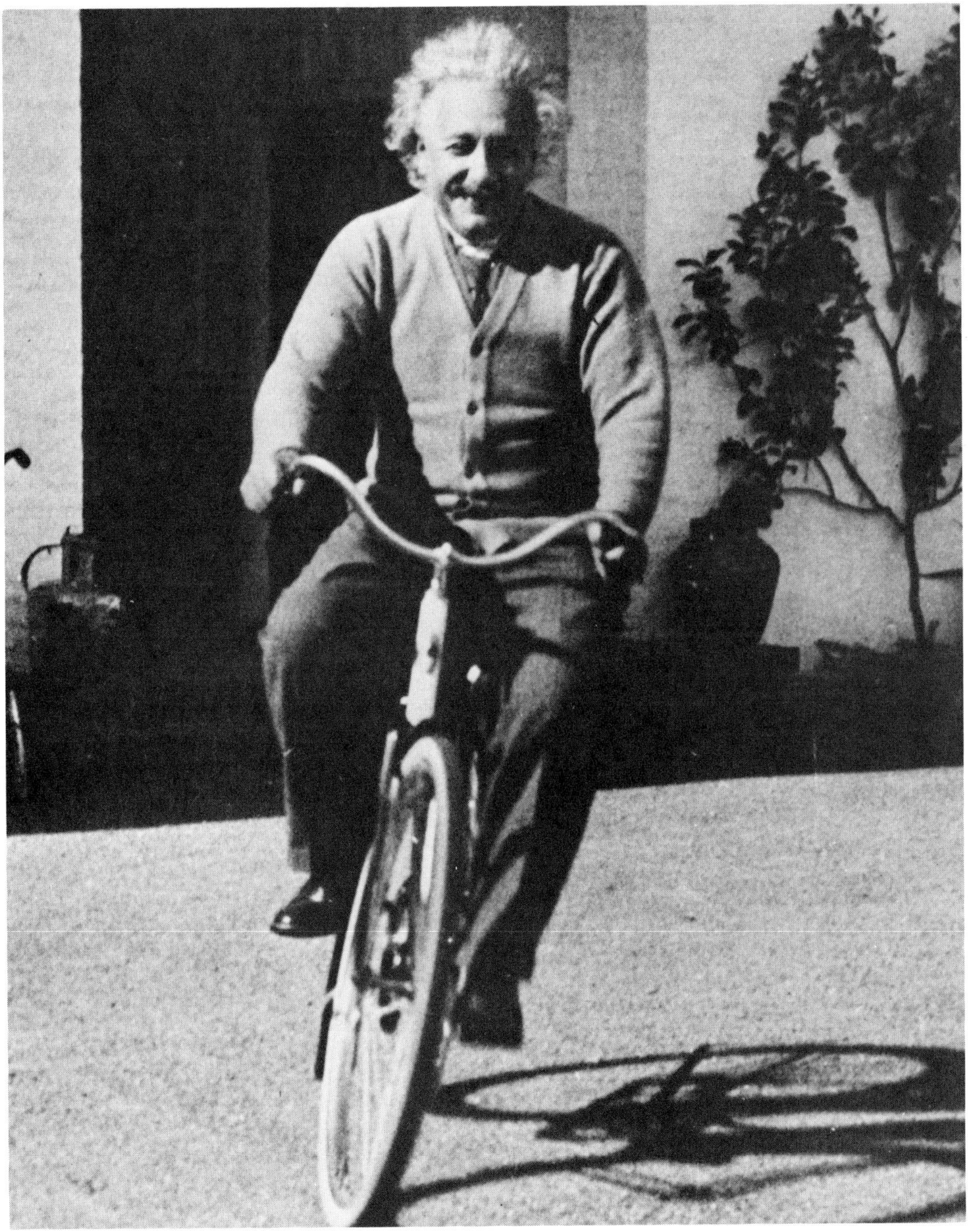

> "Absolute, true, and mathematical time of itself and by its own nature, flows uniformly, without regard to anything external."
>
> Sir Isaac Newton

> "People like us, who believe in physics, know that the distinction between past, present, and future is only a stubbornly persistent illusion."
>
> Albert Einstein

perceptions differ. A better alternative is to know the universe relatively, to know what and where a thing is compared to another thing at a particular time. Einstein's theories showed the world how to see and measure one event relative to another.

In 1905, Einstein published the Special Theory of Relativity. Part of his theory is the idea of space-time, which he called the *fourth dimension*. Another part of his Special Relativity theory is the theory of mass-energy, known today by the formula $E = mc^2$. Einstein called each idea a special theory because together they formed part of a larger theory.

In 1916, Einstein published the General Theory of Relativity, a more complete theory about the universe. It shows more complex interrelationships of time, space, mass, energy, motion, and gravity. Its complex formulas can measure and predict events at great distances occurring at high speeds. In General Relativity, Einstein introduced the concepts of gravitational fields and curved space.

From the time of publication, Einstein acknowledged that his theories were incomplete because atomic events could not be fitted together into a unified whole and because his theories could not predict events at the outer limits of the universe.

The Mystery of Einstein

Special and General Relativity proved that the mystery of the universe is still unsolved. How could one man develop a new order, or design, for the entire universe? Who was Albert Einstein? How did he arrive at this new perception? What exactly is the new underlying idea about space and time, mass and energy, gravitational force and curved space that is called Relativity?

How one man's mind could produce a new view of the universe will perhaps always be a mystery. But events in Einstein's childhood explain how he became interested in physics and mathematics. He had a curious mind, and he asked many questions; in particular he asked questions about a compass, geometry, and light.

When Einstein was a five-year-old child sick in bed,

his father gave him a compass. Einstein wanted to know why the needle always pointed north. His father told him that a magnetic field surrounds the earth, a space in which an invisible force attracts objects, as a magnet attracts. The needle responds to this invisible force. In his "Autobiographical Notes," written when Einstein was sixty-seven, he said that he remembered how he had thought an invisible field must be a "miracle," that "something deeply hidden had to be behind things." Later when he was in grade school, someone gave him a book about Euclid's geometry. Einstein was fascinated with geometry, and he read and studied the whole book. When he was twelve he asked his teacher, "What would a light beam look like if you traveled along beside it?" The teacher said it would appear to be at rest; it would look as if it were standing still. Einstein seemed doubtful.

When he was sixteen and in his final year of school in Aarau, Switzerland, he discovered a book that helped him answer these questions, but it provoked his curiosity even more. The book described Scottish physicist James Clerk Maxwell's theory about light, which was based on work done by Michael Faraday, an English scientist.

When Einstein learned about the Faraday and Maxwell experiments as well as experiments by scientists named Michelson and Morley, his childhood questions about a compass and light beam were answered. But the information from these experiments had further significance because the discoveries were basic to Einstein's later relativity theories.

Einstein as a boy, with his sister Maja.

Mysterious Forces

Faraday made observations about the attracting power of a magnet. From his experiments, Faraday found that both attracting and repelling forces were in the air around a magnet. These forces occur because a magnet has positive and negative charges, or forces. Faraday found that the combination of a positive and a negative force attracts, but two positive forces, or two negative forces, repel, or push each other away. The area around a magnet where the air is filled with magnetic forces is called a field.

Top: James Clerk Maxwell. Bottom: Michael Faraday. The ideas of these two men provoked Einstein's curiosity.

In 1865, Maxwell, an expert mathematician, devised equations based on Faraday's findings. Maxwell showed that both electricity and magnets have positive and negative charges, or forces; in other words, electricity and magnetism are two varieties of a single force, which he called electromagnetism. Maxwell showed, in addition, that light is a variety of that force as well. For Einstein, reading Maxwell's theory was "like a revelation." Now he understood what his father had meant when he said the compass had a magnetic field. The force and field concepts are basic parts of Einstein's General Relativity theory.

Einstein's question about the light beam was answered by Maxwell's equations and by an experiment conducted in the 1800s by two Americans—Albert Michelson, a physicist, and Edward Morley, a chemist. In ancient times, Aristotle had said that a substance he called *aether* filled all the space between planets and stars. He thought *aether* transmitted light. Michelson and Morley tested Aristotle's theory. They sent two light beams into space, still thinking it was *aether*. They sent one beam against the wind, or *aether* drift, and one across it. They expected to find that the beam traveling against the *aether* drift traveled slower. It did not, and Michelson and Morley, as well as other scientists, thought the experiment was flawed. But not Einstein. To him, Maxwell's equations and the Michelson-Morley experiment proved that light travels at a constant speed, always at 186,000 miles per second, and that *aether* does not exist. Einstein now knew that a light beam would travel faster than he would; his teacher was wrong. The constant speed of light, represented as "c" in mathematical formulas, became the measuring standard in Einstein's equations.

Einstein's curious mind led him to further thoughts about the universe and created in him an urge to solve some of its mysteries. In "Autobiographical Notes," Einstein told about the wonder in his young mind. He said, "Out yonder there was this huge world, which exists independently of us human beings and which stands before us like a great, eternal riddle, at least partially accessible to our inspection and thinking. The contemplation of this world beckoned.... The mental grasp of this extrapersonal world...swam as the highest aim half consciously and half unconsciously before my mind's eye."

After graduating from Zurich Polytechnic Institute in Zurich, Switzerland, in 1900, Einstein took a job reviewing patents for new inventions. He moved to Bern, Switzerland. The job suited him because it left time between customers to think about this huge world "out yonder" and to solve some part of its "great eternal riddle." By 1905, when he was twenty-six years old, he had solved four riddles; he had developed four theories, which he published in volume 17 of *Annalen der Physik*, a German scientific publication. The Special Theory of Relativity was one of them.

Special Relativity

An explanation of Special Relativity is easier to follow if the terms "event" and "frame of reference" are clarified first. An *event* is something that takes place at a single point in space at a specified point in time. It refers to many kinds of happenings in science. A spaceship accelerating, an electron changing orbits, a stone falling—all these are events. A *frame of reference* is the position or place from which an observer views or studies an event. For example, one can view a football play from row five on the fifty-yard line; that is one frame of reference. Or one can view the play from the press box high above the action on the field; that is a different frame of reference. In the Special Relativity theory, one frame of reference is moving; the other is not.

Special Relativity is a theory about motion, space, and time. It makes these claims:

- There is no observable, absolute motion; only relative motion is observable.
- The velocity of light is constant and not affected by the motion of its source.
- Time is relative, not absolute.
- Space and time are interdependent; that is, they are dependent on each other and form a four-dimensional continuum.

The theory provides mathematical calculations for

Here is part of Einstein's discussion of his theory of relativity, as published in the German scientific journal *Annalen der Physik*.

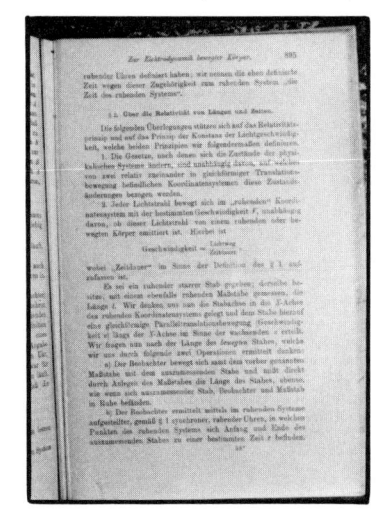

> "Hardly anyone who has truly understood this theory [of General Relativity] will be able to resist being captivated by its magic."
>
> Albert Einstein

> "Perhaps relativity, too, will have to be corrected eventually for increasingly large phenomena, just as it has corrected Newtonian mechanics."
>
> David Bergamini, *The Universe*

measuring an event moving in one direction at a steady speed relative to, or compared to, an event not moving. In addition, the theory provides arguments or illustrations to support the above claims.

Einstein showed that there is no reliable standard for measuring either space or time. Because there is no reliable standard for space and time, there is no accurate way to measure the size, shape, and location of a single object in space. Neither is there an accurate way to measure when an event occurs and the amount of time taken up by an event. A better way, he argued, is to measure an event from one frame of reference in relation to another.

In a book called *Relativity: The Special and General Theory*, published first in 1920, Einstein explained these arguments and used a moving train to illustrate them.

Einstein told stories about a very long train moving at a uniform speed on very long, straight tracks. One observer, M^1, rode on the train; the other observer, M, stood on the embankment near the tracks. Einstein marked off two spots along the tracks and identified them as A and B. He made a diagram like this:

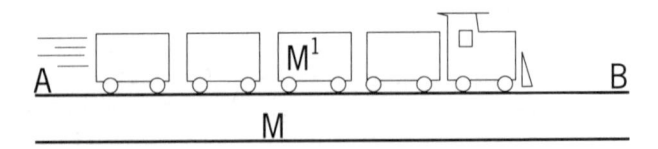

Relative Motion, Space, and Time

One story illustrates how measurements change for motion or speed: Just as the train car in which M^1 is riding passes in front of M on the embankment, M^1 walks from the back of the train car to the front. How fast is M^1 moving? Because M^1 is moving at the same speed as the train, he feels he is moving no faster than his walking speed. M, however, sees him traveling at the speed of the train plus his walking speed. Therefore, two measurements exist for the same event.

A second example illustrates how measurements

for space change. Einstein defined space in a concrete way by saying it is what we measure with measuring rods, or rulers. If M^1 measured a window in the train car, its dimensions would be the same as they would be when the train is at rest. But M on the embankment would see a window in motion. Because the train is speeding forward, the window appears shorter to M. The front vertical edge appears moved toward the back vertical edge, as if the window were squeezed together. That space is what M sees in his reality. Again there are two measurements for the same space taken from two frames of reference.

A third example illustrates different measurements for time from the two frames of reference. Imagine two lightning strikes occurring at the same time, one at point A and one at point B. Imagine also that M, situated midway between the two points, is equipped with giant mirrors set up at angles for him to see both strikes at once. Because M is not moving, the lightning strikes appear via the mirrors to occur at the same time. M^1 continues his forward motion on the train toward B, and the light from B reaches him before the light from A reaches him. Therefore, M^1 concludes that the lightning struck at B first. Each frame of reference produced different time measurements. Einstein said, "Unless we are told the reference-body [the

Einstein stated that the width of a train window would be different to a person sitting beside it than to a person viewing it as the train travels by.

When lightning strikes, a person closer to it would say it struck at an earlier time than would a person farther away.

place] to which the statement of time occurs, there is no meaning in a statement of the time of an event." In other words, time has meaning only in relationship to a place, or a space.

A fourth example illustrates another difference in time measurement. Einstein defined time in a specific way by saying it is what we measure with clocks. Consider the problem of measuring the time it takes for the front edge of the train to travel from point A to point B. On the embankment, M stands at A and marks the time on one clock when the front edge of the train passes A. An assistant stands at B and marks the time on another clock when the front edge passes B. By comparing the time on the two clocks, M can determine the amount of time the train took to pass from A to B. From a different frame of reference, M^1 uses his clock to mark the passages at A and at B. His time, it seems, should match the time that M found. But Einstein said the two measurements would differ. In *Relativity*, he said, "As a consequence of its motion the clock goes more slowly than when at rest." If the clock goes more slowly, less time seems to pass. (As difficult as this may be to believe, the difference in the speed at which clocks run while moving and not moving has been proven by experiment.)

Light as the Key

These examples show that one motion has two speeds, one space has two sets of dimensions, and one event seems to occur at different times. With these many differences, how can an object or an event be measured accurately? The answer lies in the velocity, or speed, of light. Because light has a constant speed, it can be used with two sets of measurements to calculate a relationship between the two. At 186,000 miles per second, light has a velocity that "can neither be reached nor exceeded by any real body," said Einstein. Consequently, all measured speeds of real objects will be less than 186,000 miles per second.

To accurately measure one event relative to another, Einstein began with two sets of measurements, one for M^1, which was moving, and one for M, which was not moving. He explained that an event can be identified by three spatial dimensions—length, width, and height—and by the time the event occurred. An event for M, not moving, can be identified with three space measurements and one time measurement. An event for M¹, moving, can be identified by its own set of three space measurements and one time measurement. Once the two sets are established, the constant *c*, the speed of light, can be used to show how the two sets are related.

In summary, Einstein said that since neither space nor time is absolute, they change depending on where they are measured from. Thus, we get inaccurate measurements when we try to measure events separately. A better way is to measure an event in a particular space at a particular time from two frames of reference and relate the two. Also,

- Because time is one of the four co-ordinates or dimensions used for measuring, it is the fourth dimension.
- Because both an event's space—measured in length, width, and height—and its time are measured, the result is a measurement of *space-time*.
- Because the calculations show an event's space in relation to time, it is a theory of relativity.
- Because the theory measures only uniform, even motion and not all motion, it is a partial, or special, theory of relativity.

"It Is" or "It Depends"?

Regarding space and time, two little sentences seem to sum up the difference between Newtonian thought and relativity. Newton seemed to say, "It is"; Einstein seemed to say, "It depends." Newton would look at the train and say there are constant measurements of its speed, location, and size. Einstein would say these measurements change depending on where they are measured from. When Max Planck, the editor of the science publication *Annalen der Physik,* read Einstein's paper on Special Relativity, he called Einstein "the Copernicus of the twentieth century." Just as Copernicus had introduced a new solution to the mystery of the universe, so too had Einstein.

There are two important points to keep in mind about this Special Theory, one concerning its use and

According to Einstein's theory, even time is relative.

Newton (left) believed that the space and time of an object are always the same; Einstein (right) believed they are different, depending on where and when they are being experienced.

the other its limits. First, Einstein said the theory should be used not for trains but for speeds that more closely approach the speed of light. Newton's laws predict accurately enough for trains and apples and planets, but relativity works better for greater speeds and greater distances.

Second, the theory is limited. Einstein tried from 1908 to 1912 to work gravity into the Special Theory, but he never could. Further, the Special Theory works only for objects at rest or in *uniform* motion. When engineers accelerate trains or apply the brakes, the theory no longer works. This is one reason Einstein later developed the General Theory of Relativity. He wanted a theory that included gravity and events in non-uniform motion.

$E = mc^2$

In 1905, in addition to the paper on space-time, Einstein also published a paper on a theory about the way mass and energy are related. The theory is known as $E=mc^2$, a theory he included with his Special Relativity theory. An explanation of $E=mc^2$ is easier to follow if the terms "mass" and "energy" are clarified first. *Mass* is not exactly the size and weight of an object, although those qualities are related. Mass is a concept about the density of an object. A small, heavy object like a lead ball is more dense than a small, light object like a styrofoam ball. Mass is a number representing density, calculated from an object's size and weight. *Energy* is a source of power that generates an action or a reaction. Burning causes heat, which is a source of power. Moving water also creates energy and is a source of power. In our world, any change in an object's speed, location, or composition requires energy. In $E=mc^2$, Einstein's theory refers to all mass and all energy, not a particular kind of energy.

The mass-energy part of Special Relativity is a theory about the way mass and energy transform, or convert, into one another. The theory makes these claims:

1) The mass of a body in motion is a function of the energy content and varies with the velocity. In other words, how much mass a moving object has depends on the energy it acquires from the speed of its motion.

2) Matter and energy are equivalent; that is, matter can change into energy and energy can change in-

Einstein's theory of relativity is unable to measure things that are not in constant motion (traveling at the same constant speed). If the object speeds up (accelerates) or slows down (decelerates), the theory does not work.

These two balls are the same size, but their masses are very different. The styrofoam ball is less dense; it has air pockets combined with its plastic matter; it has less mass. The lead ball appears to be solid; it is denser and has more mass.

Einstein is best known to many people for devising the formula $E=mc^2$. Here the famous equation has been superimposed on a photograph of the interior of a nuclear reactor, its technology made possible, in part, by Einstein's theories.

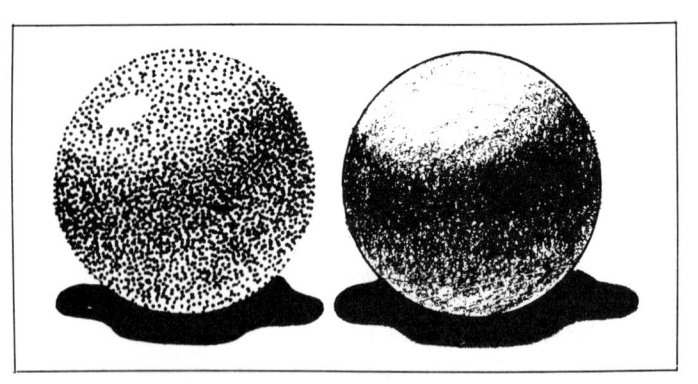

to matter. The total amount always remains equal regardless of the form.

3) No energy can be transmitted at a velocity greater than the speed of light. At great speed, near the speed of light, matter converts from one form to another, but no object can move at the speed of light or greater.

The mass-energy theory, represented by $E=mc^2$, provides mathematical calculations for measuring the amount of mass converted at speeds relative to the speed of light. In addition, the theory provides arguments for the three claims stated above.

Explanations

Einstein argued, first, that motion affects the mass of an object. He said that an object moving near the speed of light would increase in mass by taking away mass from the mechanism that put it into motion. The moving object becomes greater and the source of energy gets smaller. A familiar example showing the relationship between motion and mass is a snowball. A snowball being rolled in wet snow increases its size, its mass. We know that the snowball picks up snow from the ground and gets bigger. According to $E=mc^2$, the snowball would get bigger in a fast-moving roll by taking away mass from the person rolling the snowball. We know this event does not happen. Einstein's theory does not apply to slow, everyday events. It is true only when objects move near the speed of light.

Second, Einstein argued that mass and energy are equivalent. Before 1905, scientists thought mass and energy were two different things. Science had a law for each. The law for mass said that matter could neither be created nor destroyed, but it could be converted into different forms of matter. For example, water can freeze and be converted into ice. Likewise, the law for energy said that it could neither be created nor destroyed, even though it could be transformed into other forms of energy. For example, heat from burning coal can be transformed into electricity. After Einstein's theory, the laws had to be combined. The law now states that mass and energy may neither be created nor destroyed, but each may be converted into the other. Thus, they are equivalent.

Einstein's theory shows how that conversion can be tested and proved. He said first to measure the mass of an object and also to measure the mass of the energy source to be used to accelerate the object. Second, he said to accelerate the object to a speed near the speed of light. Third, he said to measure the mass of the accelerated object and to measure the mass of the energy source *after* it had accelerated the object. The accelerated object gets bigger and the source gets smaller by an equal amount. Because energy and mass are equivalent, the mass of the source moves to the mass of the object in high-speed motion.

When the mass of a thing is known, its energy is also known according to $E = mc^2$. In the equation, E is energy, m is mass, and c is the constant speed of light.

Although Einstein believed his theories were accurate, he thought they could never be tested because no energy source could make an object go fast enough. Our common sense tells us that familiar energies like wind and electricity are not powerful enough to reduce the mass of a fan or an electric generator and increase the mass of a feather or a toaster. Like the space-time theory, $E = mc^2$ is a theory for high-speed objects. Eventually, technology advanced so much that the theory has been tested and proven accurate. Stanford University in California has an electron accelerator that is two miles long. It was used in the 1960s to test $E = mc^2$. Electrons, tiny particles in atoms, were accelerated to travel at speeds near the speed of light. The experiments proved that the electron's mass in-

"Einstein was the most powerful mind of the twentieth century, and one of the most powerful that ever lived."

Twentieth-century philosopher
C. P. Snow

"Einstein [was] a 'lazy dog' who seldom came to class."

Hermann Minkowski, Einstein's mathematics professor at Polytechnic Institute

Einstein showed that matter and energy are equivalent; they can be converted into each other. A simple example is water (matter) being turned into heat (energy).

creased exactly as Einstein predicted it would in his theory.

Light Speed

Einstein also argued a third point. He said that no object can travel at or greater than the speed of light. At the speed of light, an energy source would disappear because its mass would convert into the moving object; at that point, all motion would stop. In *Coming of Age in the Milky Way*, Timothy Ferris told what would happen if the earth were accelerated to the speed of light. It would "contract into a two-dimensional wafer of infinite mass, on which all time would come to a stop." Today, scientists believe such an event is impossible.

The theory $E = mc^2$ gives us the mathematical calculations for the conversion of mass and energy of objects moving near the speed of light. An electron in an accelerator traveling at 90 percent the speed of light increases its mass to twice its original mass.

How can it be true, one wonders, that mass and energy are equivalent? How does this conversion happen? Atoms, tiny bundles of mass and energy that make up everything in the universe, make it possible. The atom has a mass in its center, and it has electromagnetic energy. Because its parts move and rearrange themselves and change form, it is possible that mass and energy are equivalent. Knowledge about

The Stanford Linear Accelerator, operated by Stanford University in California for the U.S. Department of Energy. The long, straight "road" heading toward the top of the picture is the two-mile-long accelerator.

atoms shows that any object is like energy bound up, like energy made solid. (Chapter 4 explains atoms and the theories about the way they work.)

In summary, Special Relativity has two parts. One part is a theory relating space and time; another part is a theory relating mass and energy. Both parts make up Einstein's Special Theory of Relativity; both parts use light as a constant in order to get one measurement for two things that are relative to one another.

By itself, Special Relativity does not make a new design for the universe, but the two theories solve parts of the mystery in new ways. Space-time is both new and old. The calculations are new, but the dual perspective of time and space is as old as the Psalms and Job. Mass-energy also is both new and old. Again, the calculations and experiments are new, but the idea that one thing becomes another is as old as primitive magic and the practice of pricking an image to harm an enemy.

General Relativity

General Relativity more closely resembles a new design for the universe than Special Relativity does. Heinz Pagels in *The Cosmic Code* calls the General Theory Einstein's greatest accomplishment because it brought motion, magnetic fields, energy, time, light, and space into a single theory. In the General Theory all parts are interrelated, not just space and time or mass and energy. Each part affects every other part. The theory indeed makes us think in new ways. It is a mystery of interconnections.

An explanation of General Relativity is easier to follow if the terms "gravitational field" and "curved," or "warped," space are clarified first. Einstein used *gravitational field* instead of *gravity*. Gravity seems like a line of force that pulls an object toward the center of the earth. Einstein said that a gravitational field of electromagnetic energy surrounding a body, such as the earth, is the same as a magnetic field surrounding a magnet. Gravity is not a *line* of force but an area, a field, of force. *Curved space* describes a shape made when a light beam travels through a gravitational field. Unimpeded light travels in a straight line, but a light beam is affected when it comes within the influence of a gravitational field; it bends to follow the force of the field. Since the gravitational field surrounding the earth, for example, follows the curvature of the earth, the light beam follows the earth's field in a curved line. The shape defined by this line is called curved, or *warped*, space.

General Relativity can predict the path of moving bodies in space-time. The theory predicts accurately because it relates motion, gravity, mass, time, light, and space to the concept of gravitational field. The theory makes this claim:

> The presence of matter results in a "warping" of the space-time continuum, so that a body in motion passing nearby will describe a curve, this being the effect known as gravitation, as evidenced by the deflection

A light beam projected from earth will not travel in a straight line. It will curve around stars and other celestial bodies because of the way their gravitational fields "warp" space.

of light rays passing through a gravitational field. In other words, the presence of a body of matter, like a planet, creates a gravitational field and causes an object passing near it to follow the curve of its field. The curving of light rays is evidence of the gravitational field.

The theory provides a new geometry to calculate all of the related parts. In addition, Einstein provided arguments to show the interrelationship of the parts that make up the theory. Let us look now at Einstein's six arguments.

First, Einstein argued that non-uniform or changing motion is like a gravitational field. In other words, motion that speeds up or slows down has the same effect as gravity. Einstein told a story about a person floating weightless in a spaceship. If the spaceship were suddenly pulled upward, accelerated, the floor of the spaceship would rise and hit the rider's feet and keep her feet on the floor as long as the spaceship accelerated. When the spaceship hit the rider's feet, the impact would feel the same as if she had jumped to the ground. If the spaceship had no windows, the person would be unable to distinguish between acceleration and gravity.

Another example is about M^1 riding on the train. If the engineer suddenly applied the brakes when M^1 did not expect it, his body would be thrust forward. Even though his body moves horizontally, the feeling of motion is not unlike the feeling of falling. Increasing or decreasing speed resembles gravity, or the power in a gravitational field.

Second, Einstein argued that what we have come to think of as gravity is really a gravitational field much like a magnetic field surrounding a magnet. According to Newton, a stone falls to the earth because the earth's mass attracts the stone directly. According to Einstein, the earth does not attract the stone directly; instead, the earth has a gravitational field, like an electromagnetic field; if the stone comes within that field, the field acts on the stone and makes it fall.

Third, Einstein argued that inertial, unmoving, mass is equal to gravitational mass. Inertial mass has to

Albert Einstein at his desk in the patent office in Bern, Switzerland.

This diagram shows Galileo's ball-dropping experiment done in outer space. In space there is no gravity; therefore, as long as the spaceship is still or moves at a constant rate of motion, the balls (and Galileo) would float freely rather than fall. But if the spaceship speeds up, the acceleration acts like gravity. The balls (and Galileo) would appear to fall just as they would on earth.

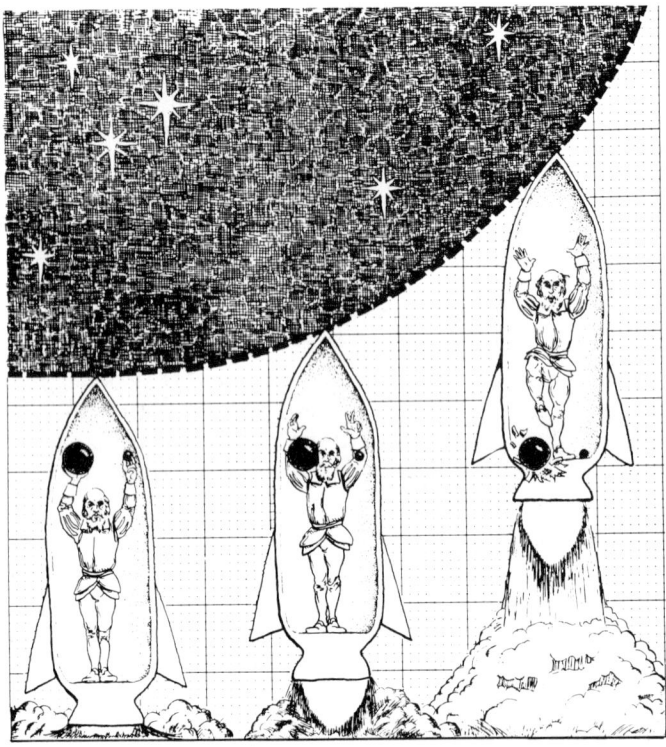

do with the amount of energy it takes to move or to stop a body. It relates to Newton's law that says a body will stay at rest (remain inert) unless acted on by a force or will continue to move unless acted on.

Think back to the bowling ball. Visualize it sitting on a little stand to prevent its rolling. The amount of effort needed to push it across the floor on its stand is its inertial mass; the amount of effort needed to lift it is its gravitational mass. Einstein said the two are equal. A relationship exists between inertial and gravitational mass.

Time and Gravity

Fourth, Einstein argued that a gravitational field affects a clock just as motion affects a clock. In his book *Relativity*, Einstein said that a rotating clock marks time more slowly than a clock that is standing still. He went on to say that "in every gravitational field, a clock will go more or less quickly, according to the position in which the clock is situated." A clock runs slower in a strong gravitational field just as it runs slower when it has greater motion.

He told a story about two people sitting on a giant rotating disk, both watching the clocks beside them. One sat at the very center where there was no rotating motion. The other person sat at the edge of the disk and rotated with it. The clock at the edge moved slower. Einstein concluded that it is impossible to obtain an absolute definition of time with clocks.

Another story illustrates the effect that increased velocity and a strong gravitational field have on clocks. Timothy Ferris wrote about an imaginary astronaut leaving for a long space trip right after high school graduation. Imagine that she traveled in a spaceship at a speed 90 percent of the velocity of light, at 167,400 miles per second. She traveled for twenty years; during that time at that speed, her clock moved one-half as fast as her classmates' clocks at home. When she arrived for her twentieth class reunion, she was the youngest person from her class. Both stories illustrate the relativity of time and the effect motion and gravitation have on clocks. The second story illustrates *how much* effect motion and gravitation have on time and clocks.

Fifth, Einstein argued that gravitation affects the way light travels. Einstein said, "in general, rays of light are propagated [transmitted] curvilinearly [in a curved line] in gravitational fields." When we use a flashlight, its beam looks straight because it is short. Imagine two laser light beams projected into space. Einstein said they would be transmitted curvilinearly in the earth's gravitational field; that is, they would bend to follow the earth's surface. We can imagine the two parallel beams traveling like railroad tracks around the earth at the equator and eventually meeting. According to this idea, each body in the universe would cause light to curve dependent on its gravitational field. For example, a smaller body, like the moon, would have a different curve from the planet Neptune, a large planet.

Warped Space

Sixth, Einstein argued that a gravitational field

"Science is a response to the demand that our experience places upon us, and what we are given in return by science is a new human experience—seeing with our mind the internal logic of the cosmos."

Heinz Pagels, *The Cosmic Code*

"In the last analysis, magic, religion, and science are nothing but theories of thought."

Theodore H. Gaster, *The New Golden Bough*

"Nature and Nature's laws
    lay hid in night:
God said, *Let Newton be!*
    and all was light."

Seventeenth-century English poet
Alexander Pope

"It did not last: the Devil
    howling 'Ho!
Let Einstein be!' restored
    the status quo."

Twentieth-century poet J. C. Squire

curves, or warps, space. An object floating in space would follow the curved space in a planet's gravitational field.

Einstein found in working on the General Relativity Theory that the concept of curved space required a new mathematics in order to do the calculations. The geometry Einstein studied as a boy was developed by Euclid several centuries B.C.; it was developed for flat, not curved, surfaces. Einstein illustrated the problem of calculating for curved space with a story. He told about a flat marble table, marked off in squares, all touching as on a chessboard. If the center were heated, it would expand and the squares would change shape as the table forms a dome in the center. The dome would illustrate the curved space of a gravitational field. The squares would change to look like this:

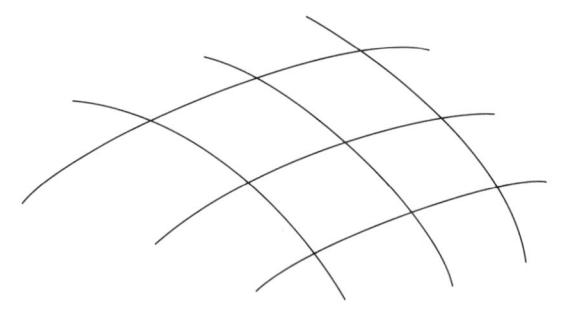

Einstein solved the mathematical problem of measuring curved space by using calculations originated by another mathematician and then modifying them for his theory. This mathematics was a new geometry.

General Relativity is a complex theory and its mathematical calculations are difficult. They have been tested, and the theory worked as Einstein predicted it would. Einstein predicted that the sun's gravitational field would bend or curve light coming from a nearby star. He said the starlight would be deflected an angle of 1.75 seconds of an arc (part of a curve used for measuring)—enough bending to be measured. On May 29, 1919, Arthur Eddington, a British astronomer, went to Brazil to test Einstein's prediction during an eclipse, the only time a star's light

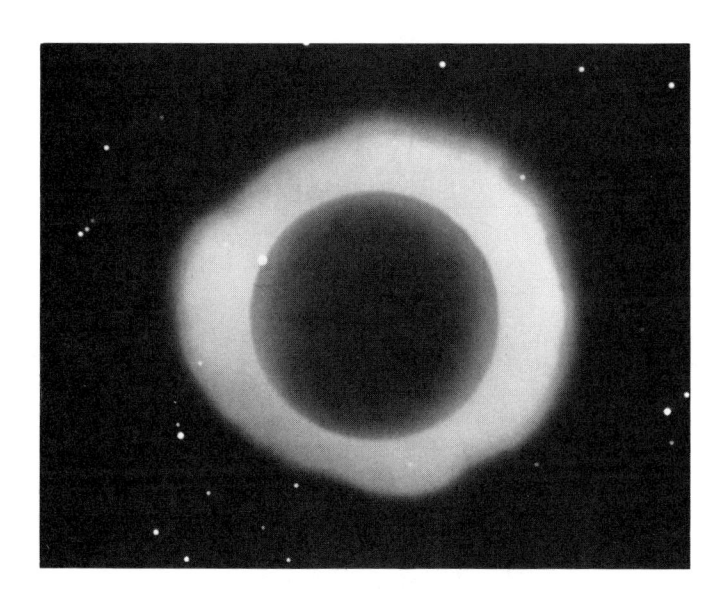

During an eclipse of the sun (left), Arthur Eddington (right) proved Einstein's idea that the sun's gravitational field would bend the light of a star.

can be seen near the sun. He measured a star's position at the time of the eclipse and again six months later when the star was not near the sun. The experiment confirmed that the star's light bent around the sun's gravitational field exactly in the amount Einstein had said it would. When Einstein learned of the news, he was not surprised. "The theory is correct," he said.

Newton's laws of gravity are still used for smaller distances and weak gravitational fields, but only Einstein's General Theory works for strong gravitational fields, massive bodies, and vast distances. It is an amazing theory.

The Limitations of Relativity

As complete a design as General Relativity is, Einstein acknowledged that it has limitations. It is limited because it does not take into account the workings of the atom, the topic of chapter 4. Also, the theory does not solve the problem of the future of the universe. According to General Relativity, the universe is expanding; that is, stars are moving outward in space away from the earth and each other. What will eventually happen to them? There are two theories: They will keep moving outward in space infinitely, or they will stop. Einstein predicted that the universe will con-

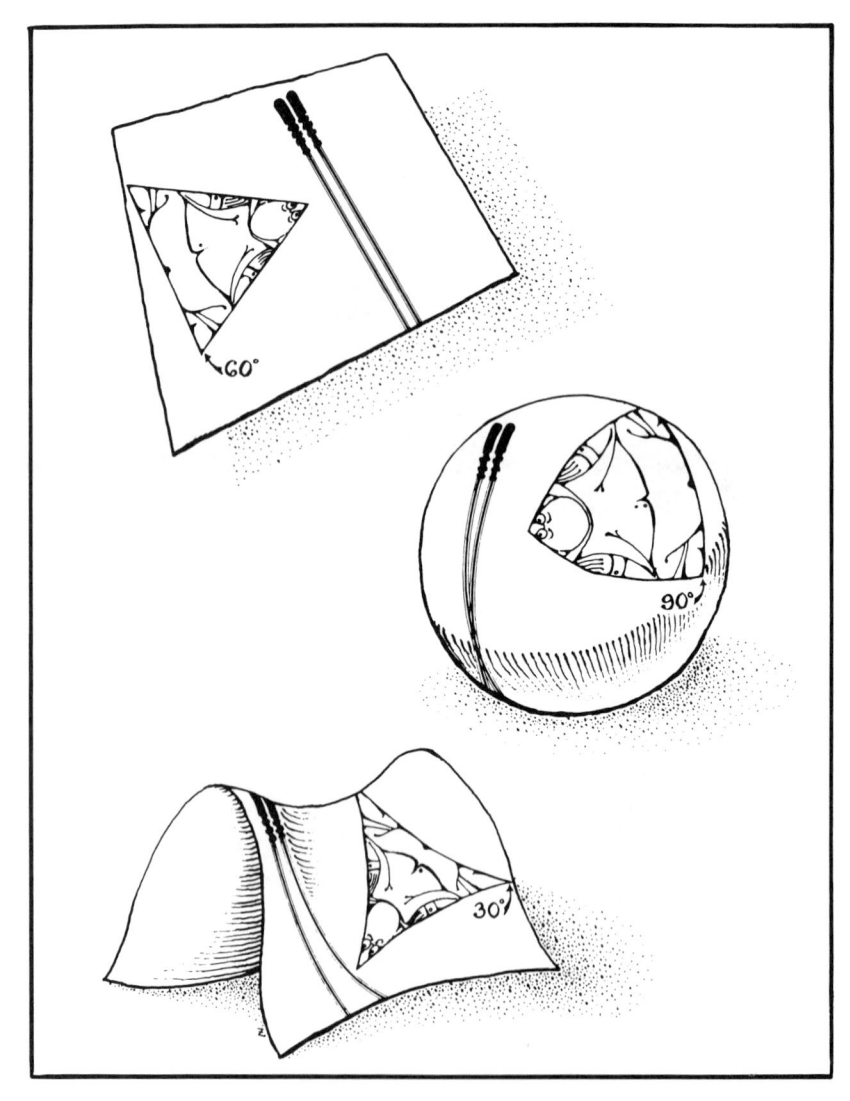

Three concepts of the universe. Top: To people who thought the earth was flat, the universe might have looked like this. Parallel light beams would travel into space, never meeting, and a flat body (like the equilateral triangle) would be undistorted. Middle: Einstein believed the universe is a closed system. He thought the universe would expand as long as energy would allow it and then it would contract. Light beams would come together and cross, and a flat body would puff out convexly. Bottom: Other theorists think the universe is an open system; it will continue spreading in a non-uniform way. Light beams would diverge and a flat body would distort with the curves of space.

tinue to expand until no more energy remains to propel stars outward. It will then stop and reverse its movement and contract in a reverse pattern. His idea is referred to as a *closed universe* because it describes an outer limit beyond which the universe cannot expand. Other scientists believe the opposing idea of infinite expansion. This idea is called an *open universe* because the stars move out into open space infinitely.

Two light beams projected into space can illustrate the two opposing ideas. Imagine projecting the two light beams into outer space in parallel lines. If they could be seen at the outer limit of the universe, they would no longer be parallel. If the universe is closed, as Einstein thought, they would converge, or come together, and curve into a circle. If the universe is open, they would diverge, or spread apart, and form the shape of a hyperbola, a shape that looks like a saddle blanket for a sway-backed horse.

How can we imagine a universe based on relativity in which space curves around gravitational fields? Imagine a red-and-white-checked tablecloth. On earth it would lie flat on a two-dimensional tabletop. Now imagine a gigantic red-and-white-checked tablecloth stretched out across space. It would have a warp, or curve, at every place where it passed near a large mass with a gravitational field. At those places, the checks

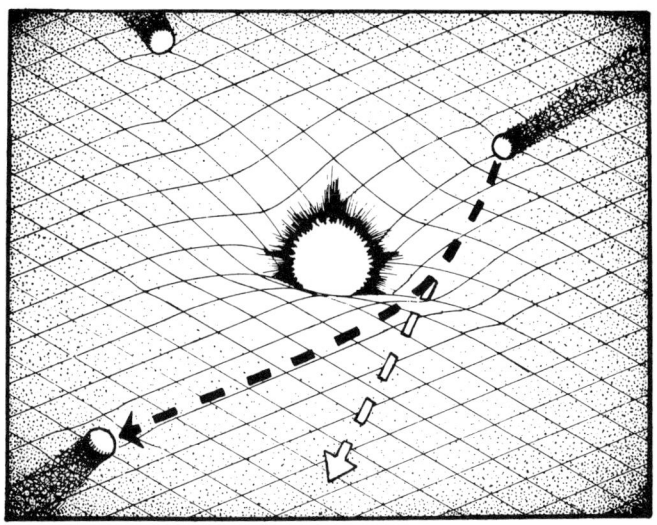

A representation of the curvature of space around the sun. Keep in mind that the earth is not a flat plane like a tablecloth; this diagram just gives an idea of what curved space is like.

Einstein's desk in the patent office, with papers containing some of his calculations.

would change shape and their lines would curve. Near the earth a part of it would be warped to fit the earth's gravitational field; near Venus another part of it would warp to fit Venus's gravitational field; near the sun another part would warp. And if it were big enough to go through the whole universe, it would curve to make its own shape. If Einstein is right and the universe is closed, it would curve into a sphere. If others are right and the universe is open, it would take the shape of a saddle blanket. Today we do not know the fate of the universe, nor do we know its design at the outer limits. It is still a mystery.

The Mystery of a Vast Universe

Other important theories about the design of the universe resulted from pieces contributed by several people, but Einstein alone solved the mystery of relativity. He described what started him on the General Theory. He said, "I was sitting in a chair in the patent office at Bern, when all of a sudden a thought occurred to me: 'If a person falls freely he will not feel his own weight.' I was startled. This simple thought made a deep impression on me. It impelled me toward a theory of gravitation." When he finished the theory in November of 1915, he had this to say about

Einstein teaching in France in 1922.

his work: "In all my life I have never before labored so hard.... Compared with this problem, the original [Special] Theory of Relativity is child's play." The General Theory was published the following spring in 1916.

Einstein showed the world an immense universe and the mystery of its vast and invisible curved space. Let us look next at another invisible space, another important part of the universe's design—the tiny universe of the atom. Though Einstein did not create a solution to the atom's mystery, he published two papers in 1905 that contributed theories for others to work on a solution. In one paper, he described a quanta of light. From that paper developed a branch of physics called quantum mechanics, or quantum theory. What is a quanta, and what is the mystery of the atom?

Four

The Building Blocks

With his theories of relativity, Einstein led the twentieth century to a new underlying idea for the universe. His design gave us the fourth dimension, space-time, gravitational fields, and curved space. Relativity expands our view of the physical universe, but it does not expand our understanding of the atom. Einstein's theories of relativity do not address a key question about the world's design: What are objects in the universe made of?

The question dates back to ancient times when the atom was first thought to be the basic building block. The ancient philosophers, Aristotle and Democritus, held opposing viewpoints about the atom. Aristotle thought matter could be divided into smaller and smaller bits; Democritus thought the solid, grainy atom was indivisible. Democritus was wrong.

The atom is a tiny space measuring a millionth of a millionth of an inch. Imagine dividing an inch into a million parts; then imagine dividing one of those parts into a million parts. That is how small an atom is. New knowledge about the atom changed the answers to old questions about matter and light, space and motion, mass and energy. With the work of many scientists over several years, a new theory evolved describing what the atom is and how it works.

Opposite: A plexiglas model of the U-235 atom.

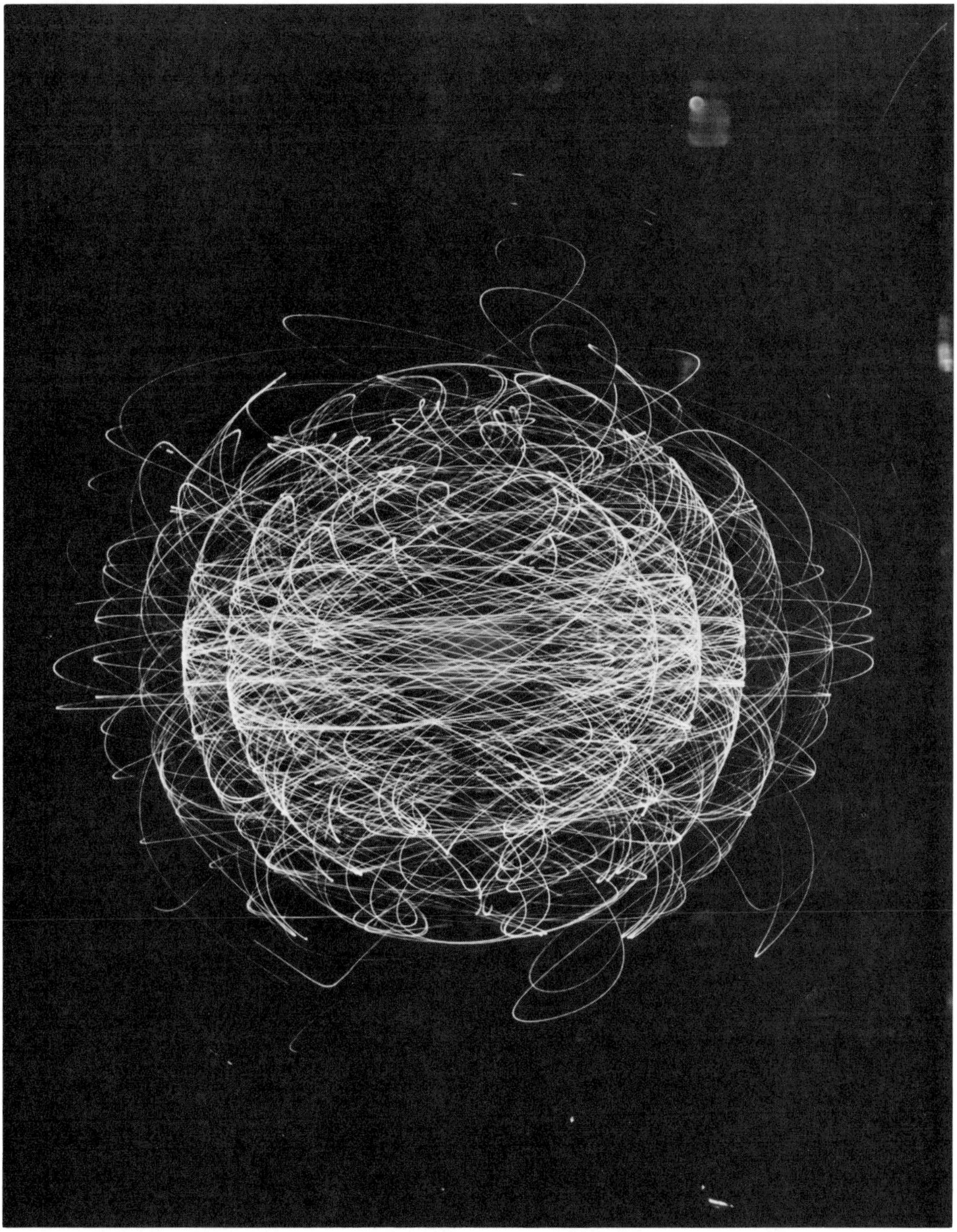

> "Physicists used to believe that they could capture all of nature in their net of mathematics."
>
> Timothy Ferris, *Coming of Age in the Milky Way*

> "There is nothing deader than an equation."
>
> Physicist John Archibald Wheeler

Twentieth-century physicists approached their search into the universe of the atom with the assumptions that had worked for centuries. They expected to discover its order and to be able to predict its events. However, their search led them to puzzling outcomes not predictable by either Newton's or Einstein's methods. While the atom's events cannot be predicted, physicists found a method of probability. *Probability* tells the statistical likelihood for an event to occur, like the probability of dice throws.

Scientists Search for Atomic Order

The search for order in the atomic world came in two stages. The first physicists proved that the atom existed. The second group of physicists searched for a working order within the atom. An exploration of the search for order in the atomic world is easier to understand if the terms naming an atom's parts are clarified first.

An *atom* is the basic part that makes up a chemical element, like oxygen or hydrogen. An atom has three main parts: a nucleus, or core; an electron particle that orbits around the nucleus; and space. The core, or nucleus, contains neutrons and protons, which are alike except for their electrical charge; a proton has a positive electrical charge and a neutron has no electrical charge (it is neutral). An atom can have as few as one proton or as many as 260 combined protons and neutrons in its nucleus. An atom also has a negatively charged particle, the electron, which orbits the nucleus. An electron orbits because its negative electrical charge and the positive electrical charge of the proton attract one another. An atom has an equal number of protons and electrons.

The rest of the atom is layers of space, described as shells, in which the electrons orbit. Electrons revolve around the nucleus in orbits, or waves. The innermost shell is a space nearest the nucleus which can have only two orbiting electrons. The second shell can have as many as eight, and the third can have eighteen. An atom with eighty-six electrons has seven shells. The outermost shell makes the outer edge of the atom.

The number of orbiting electrons (and the number

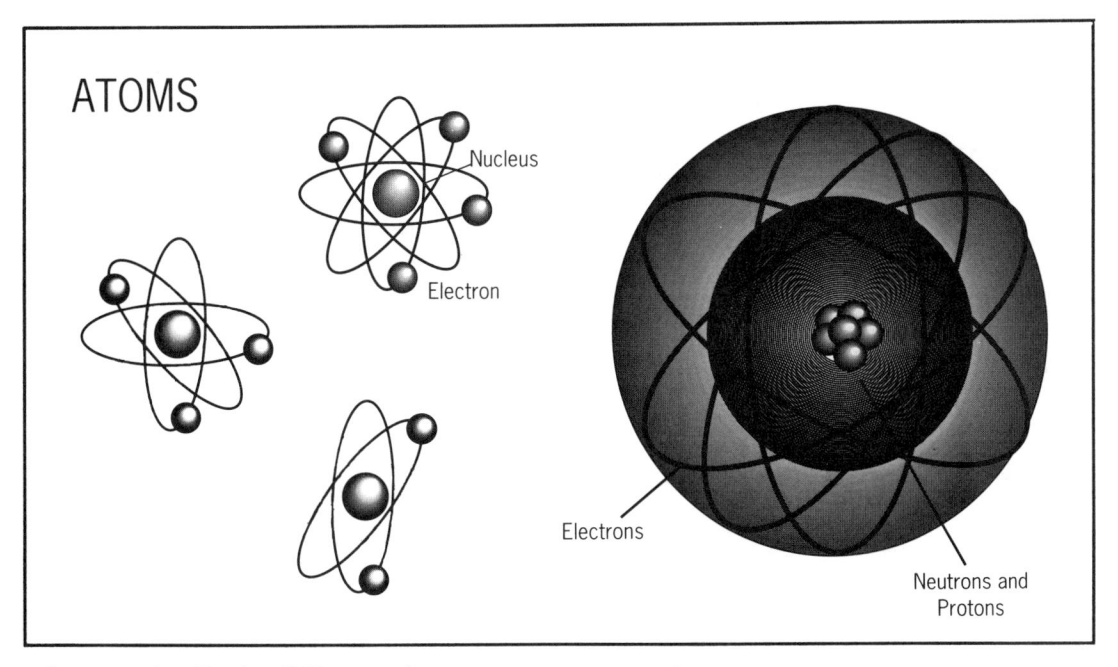

of protons) tells the difference between one atom and another. Ninety-two different kinds of atoms exist in nature, and a few others can be made in the laboratory. The names of some, besides hydrogen and oxygen, are sodium, carbon, nitrogen, copper, gold, lead, mercury, and chlorine. Hydrogen atoms are the most numerous, making up 90 percent of all atoms. Almost all living things—plants, animals, and people—are made of combinations of four elements or atoms: hydrogen, oxygen, carbon, and nitrogen. The ninety-two atoms, in multitudes of combinations, make up everything in the universe.

Light Leads to Atoms

How did scientists discover the atom and its working parts? Curiosity about light led scientists to their first discoveries. Ancient philosophers speculated that light was composed of streamers or particles or waves, but the question went unresolved until the twentieth century. Until this century, scientists thought of light as a continuum, a continuous flow. The scientists Max Planck and Albert Einstein studied light first, and then they identified the atom and proved its existence.

Left: Several different atoms, showing their nuclei and their electrons. Right: A representation of the electron "shells."

Max Planck formulated a basic energy measurement, the constant h.

Ernest Rutherford began the search to discover what is inside the atom.

In 1900 the German physicist Max Planck said that a "discrete view" of light should replace the "continuous" view: Instead of thinking of light and energy as a continuous flow, he said, it is better to think of discrete, or separate, detached parts. He thought that heat waves were emitted only in certain "packets." He called the packets *quanta*. *Quanta* is the plural of *quantum*, meaning quantity or amount. We get the name *quantum theory*, the name for the collected theories about the atom, from Max Planck.

Besides contributing the idea that energy is composed of particles, or individual units, Planck gave scientists a measuring devise, Planck's constant h. Constant h is a measuring standard for energy just as constant c is a standard for light. Planck arrived at constant h from his black-body radiation experiment.

In his black-body experiment, Planck observed the heat energy and light rays emitted from a heated metal bar. He charted his observations in numbers on a curve. When the bar was hottest, it emitted rays faster. As the bar cooled, the rays decreased in frequency (the number of rays or waves per second). The last point when light showed on the hot metal became the standard for measuring energy; that number measures an amount of energy and is called constant h. Constant h was an important first step on the road to identifying and measuring light particles and eventually atoms.

"A Rain of Particles"

In one of his papers published in 1905, Einstein took Planck's quanta idea one step farther and developed the theory of light as particles, or quanta. Einstein described light as a "rain of particles," first called *light quanta* and later called *photons*. Einstein said that when light shone on metal, the metal sent out, or emitted, one electrically charged particle, an electron, which immediately absorbed one quanta, or photon, of light. The flow of light quanta on metal and the electrons' absorbing them caused an electric current to flow, making waves. This can be compared to the way elevator doors work today. When human bodies cut off the light wave to the metal on the opposite side of the door, no current goes to the switch. As soon as the bodies leave the doorway, light again flows to the metal and creates an electric current that triggers a switch to close the door. This 1905 theory gave scientists two ideas: first, that both light and energy can be measured in quanta and, second, that light behaves both as particles and as waves. An experimenter confirmed this theory in 1923 and 1925; in 1926 Einstein received the Nobel Prize for this theory.

After energy and light had been established as quanta or particles, Einstein went on to prove that atoms exist. He combined the ideas he got from two experiments done by other scientists. In one experiment, scientists thought gas and air were composed of atoms bouncing off the ceiling, the walls, the floor, and each other in a haphazard motion, like a room full of tennis balls bouncing around. Einstein thought that observing a basketball thrown in among the tennis balls would display how the tennis balls behaved as they bombarded the basketball. In the other experiment, Robert Brown, an English botanist, had observed that pollen grains floating in water bounced around, but he did not know why. Einstein saw a connection

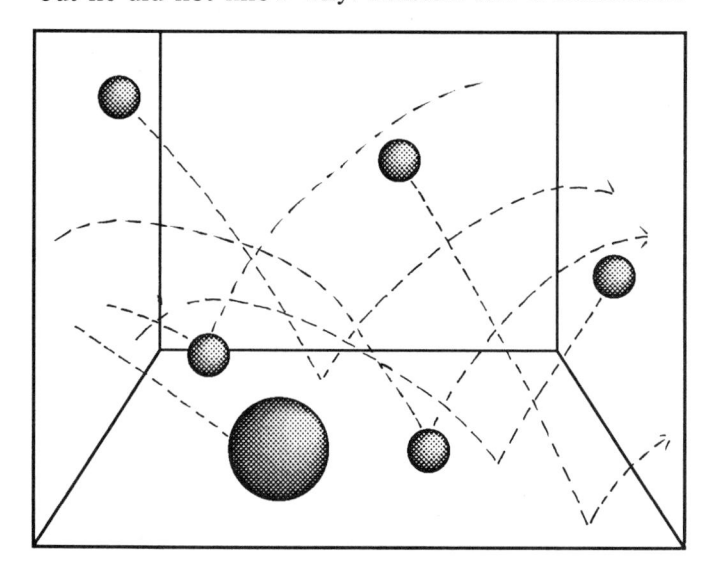

Early twentieth-century scientists thought that atoms bounced around in a sort of haphazard way, like tennis balls bouncing in a closed room. Einstein developed a way to measure this atomic motion.

between the basketball among tennis balls and the pollen grains among water atoms.

Einstein devised a mathematical method to record the motion of a pollen grain in water. He also devised a statistical method to predict its motion. (A statistical method is based on the number of times an event occurs and a prediction of the likelihood that it will occur again.) With this theory, Einstein made two important contributions to science. He found evidence that atoms exist and he created a mathematical method for charting their behavior. These were important first steps in the search for order in the atomic world.

Inside the Atom

Shortly after 1905, British physicist Ernest Rutherford performed an experiment that began to solve the mystery of what the atom contained. He discovered that the atom has a nucleus and space. He conducted an experiment using alpha rays and gold foil. He sent alpha rays, which are particles of helium nuclei, against thin gold foil. Sometimes the particles went through the gold foil, and sometimes they bounced back. Heinz Pagels in *The Cosmic Code* said the experiment was "like firing bullets at a piece of tissue paper only to find some bullets bounced backwards." Rutherford theorized that a helium nucleus in the alpha ray went through the foil when it passed through the space surrounding a gold nucleus. If a helium

Left: Ernest Rutherford is shown with another scientist in a lab. Right: Rutherford devised the gold foil experiment which confirmed the idea that space is part of an atom.

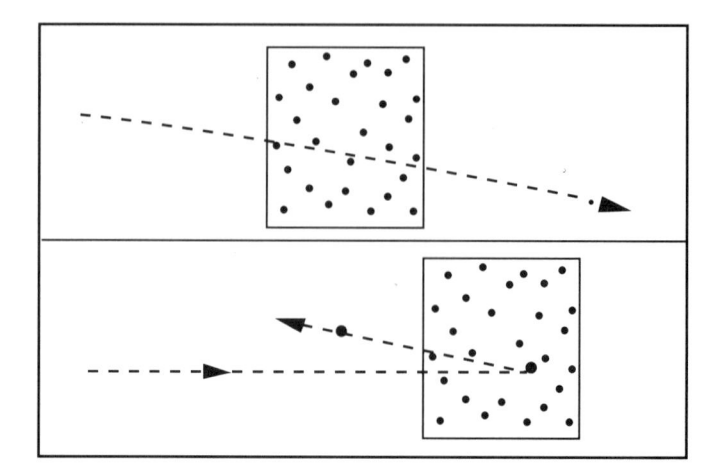

nucleus hit a gold nucleus, the helium nucleus bounced back, unable to go through. Rutherford concluded that an atom has a small nucleus, space around the nucleus, and an electron. Rutherford viewed the atom as similar to the solar system, with a nucleus, like the sun, holding the electron "planets" in orbit. (This idea was discovered later to be wrong.)

The search for order in the atomic world had reached the end of the first stage. But the complete answer to the question What are objects in the universe made of? was still a mystery because scientists did not yet know what went on inside the atom.

Scientists next tried to discover how this tiny universe works. How fast do electrons orbit? What determines the position of their orbits? How do atoms create energy? Since atoms are invisible, all experiments had to be done with rays and light and particle detectors.

Knowing the definitions of some of the terms will make the explanation of theories easier to follow. There are four important ones: "objective," "determinism," "random," and "probability." *Objective* describes an event that exists whether anyone is there to see it or not. A tree falls in a forest and a flower blooms with or without people watching. *Determinism*, a Newtonian belief, names the idea that nature and nature's laws govern or determine reality in the universe. Humans can discover the laws, but they do not make or change them. Once humans discover nature's laws, they can predict nature's events as Newton predicted the speed of falling objects. When a raindrop falls from a leaf, it falls according to nature's determined reality, independent of humans. *Indeterminacy*, the opposite, means that something is not governed by nature's laws.

Random describes events that occur according to no law or pattern whatsoever. Tossing a coin is random; either heads or tails may appear with no way to predict which it will be. Throwing dice is random; there is no way to predict which numbers will come up. In physics, events are random as long as no pattern emerges. If an observer sees a pattern, the outcome can

"Einstein never accepted that the universe was governed by chance; his feelings were summed up in his famous statement, 'God does not play dice.'"

Heinz Pagels, *The Cosmic Code*

"If God has made the world a perfect mechanism, He has at least conceded so much to our imperfect intellect that in order to predict little parts of it we...can use dice with fair success."

Scientist Max Born

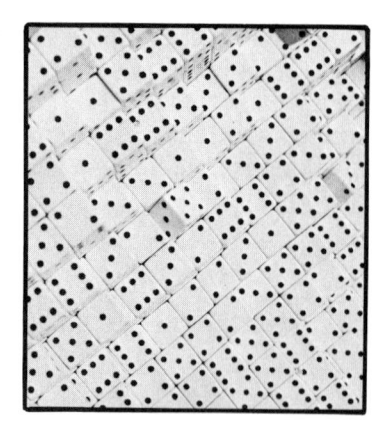

The way dice will fall when thrown cannot be absolutely predicted. But it can be guessed with percentages of probability. The table at right, for example, shows that one time out of every thirty-six throws, the dice will probably come up "snake eyes," each die showing a single dot.

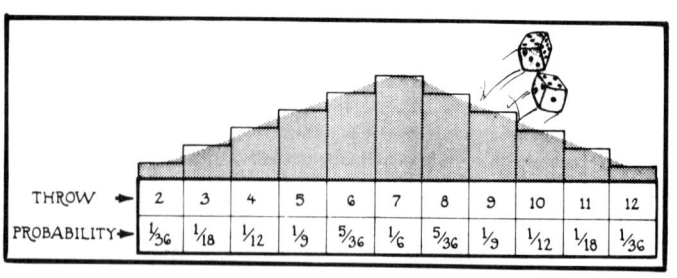

THROW	2	3	4	5	6	7	8	9	10	11	12
PROBABILITY	1/36	1/18	1/12	1/9	5/36	1/6	5/36	1/9	1/12	1/18	1/36

be predicted and the events are no longer random.

Probability describes a mathematical pattern that emerges when random events are repeated many times. With hundreds of coin tosses, heads turn up about half of the time and tails half of the time. Probability tables exist for dice throws for each number between two and twelve. Mathematical probability can tell how likely it is that a seven will be rolled, but it cannot tell what the next roll of the dice will be.

Perplexing Atoms

When physicists set out to solve the mystery of the atom, they expected to discover nature's laws that govern the objective universe of the atom. They wanted to know what laws determined the behavior of particles in the atom. Once they had discovered those laws, they thought, they could predict future behavior of the particles. They were in for a surprise. The mystery of the atom was puzzling indeed.

Atoms perplexed scientists because atomic particles did not behave the way things behave in objective, determined nature. First, scientists found that electrons had no predictable positions; they jumped around at random. An experimenter trying to identify an electron's position and speed found instead something like the old peanut-in-the-shell trick: They expected to find the electron in one position, but when they looked, it was someplace else. Furthermore, electrons did not even keep the same form; they switched from particles to waves and back to particles. They changed even while people watched. Where was nature's objectivity, scientists wondered. They named what they saw *observer-created reality*. Reality was what the observer created with the kind of experiment conducted.

Werner Heisenberg and Niels Bohr, both physicists working on the atom, discussed the problems they found. Heisenberg said, "I remember discussions with Bohr which went through many hours till very late at night and ended almost in despair; and when at the end of the discussion I went alone for a walk in the neighboring park I repeated to myself again and again the question: Can nature possibly be so absurd as it seemed to us in these atomic experiments?" Niels Bohr thought the same way. He said, "If anybody says he can think about quantum problems *without* getting giddy, that only shows he has not understood the first thing about them."

Let us look now at the theories and experiments that explored the workings of the atom to see what left physicists if not "almost in despair" then at least "giddy."

Niels Bohr and Electron Orbits

When Ernest Rutherford discovered the atom's structure, scientists thought gravity held the electrons in orbit and acceleration determined their energy. But scientists later realized that atoms would collapse according to that model: An electron accelerating would lose energy and decrease its orbital speed. The electron

Scientists Werner Heisenberg (left) and Niels Bohr (right) dine and discuss perplexing atomic questions.

would spiral into the nucleus and reduce the atom's space. As the nuclei moved together, the result would be a "dense soup." Since this does not happen, Danish scientist Niels Bohr thought electrons must orbit according to different laws, but what laws?

Bohr worked with the hydrogen atom, the simplest atom with one proton (+) and one electron (−). In 1913, he discovered that an electron's orbit is the same as a wave, a measurement distinguished by a rising and falling motion, and each orbit is equal to a complete wavelength. A hydrogen electron never orbits a part of a wavelength. Now Bohr knew why electrons do not spiral into the nucleus: They need enough room to make an orbit of a whole wavelength. This discovery is a basic idea in quantum theory.

Bohr also discovered that there are ninety-two different kinds of atoms, a discovery very important for later theories about the birth, life, and death of stars. Bohr found that when he increased the positive charge of the proton in the hydrogen nucleus by one quanta, a new electron appeared at the outer orbit. That made a new atom. An atom with two protons and two electrons is a helium atom. Adding more charges produced

Electrons travel in "waves" around the nucleus of the atom.

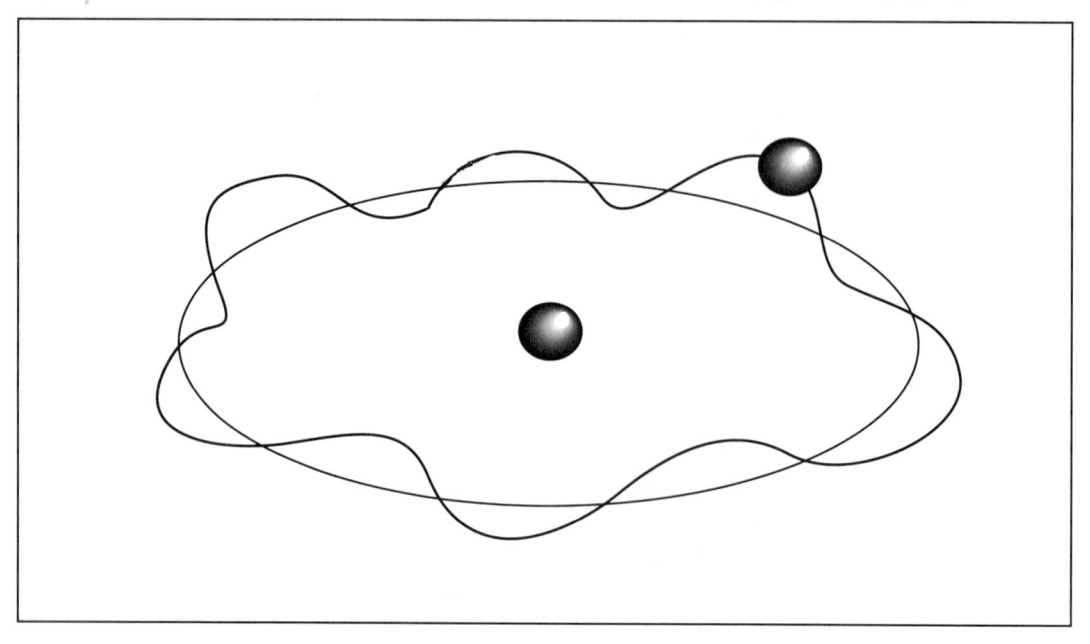

more protons and in turn produced more electrons. Each of the ninety-two natural atoms, he discovered, had its own pattern of additions of protons and electrons. The number of protons (and electrons) in an atom is called its *atomic number*. Bohr also calculated the amount of energy necessary to knock an electron out of an atom completely. He called that amount *ionization energy*. Bohr's discoveries provided three new kinds of information about the atom: that electrons jump orbits, that orbits are at least a complete wavelength, and that each of the ninety-two elements has an atomic number based on its number of protons and electrons.

The Exclusion Principle

Another physicist, Wolfgang Pauli, from Austria, discovered the *exclusion principle*, a principle that one electron excludes another electron from the same place. This theory provided more information about orbiting electrons and why the atom maintains its structure without collapsing. It states that two similar electrons cannot exist in the same place with the same velocity, or speed. If one electron has nearly the same position as another electron, they have different velocities. Electrons have negative charges, and particles with the same charge repel each other. Thus, when two negatively charged electrons get close to one another, they repel and change positions and velocities. Sometimes electrons orbiting in the outermost shells leave their own atom and orbit through two or three other atoms. If two or three atoms get close to each other, an electron in the outer orbit may get closer to the nucleus of a neighboring atom than to its own nucleus. Then the positive nucleus in the neighboring atom attracts the outer electron and the electron orbits through the neighboring atom. Electrons orbiting through neighboring atoms bind atoms into *molecules*, which are composed of two or more atoms combined. All of this whirling and jumping occurs with perfect randomness. Scientists have found no way to predict the position or velocity of an orbiting electron. This randomness made scientists "giddy," as Niels Bohr said.

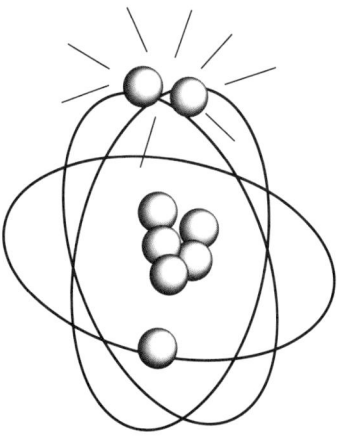

Top: Wolfgang Pauli, discoverer of the "exclusion principle." Bottom: Two electrons cannot be in the same space at the same speed. If two electrons do approach the same space, they repel each other, causing them to change direction or speed.

In 1923 French physicist Louis de Broglie proposed the idea that an electron, like a photon of light, could behave both as a particle and as a wave. This discovery made scientists "giddy" again. They were used to thinking of nature's objectivity: A flower is a flower; a tree is a tree. In the quantum world, a particle is a particle sometimes and a wave sometimes. An experiment called the two-slit experiment proved that de Broglie's idea is true.

The Two-Slit Experiment: Particles and Waves

German physicist Max Born was one of many physicists to conduct a two-slit experiment. The experiment has three phases: one for bullets, one for water waves, and one for electrons. Each phase was set up in a different room. In the first room, Born set up a miniature machine gun to shoot bullets at a screen that had two slits in it. Each slit had a door that Born could close. He set up a second screen to record the places

Max Born's two-slit experiment.

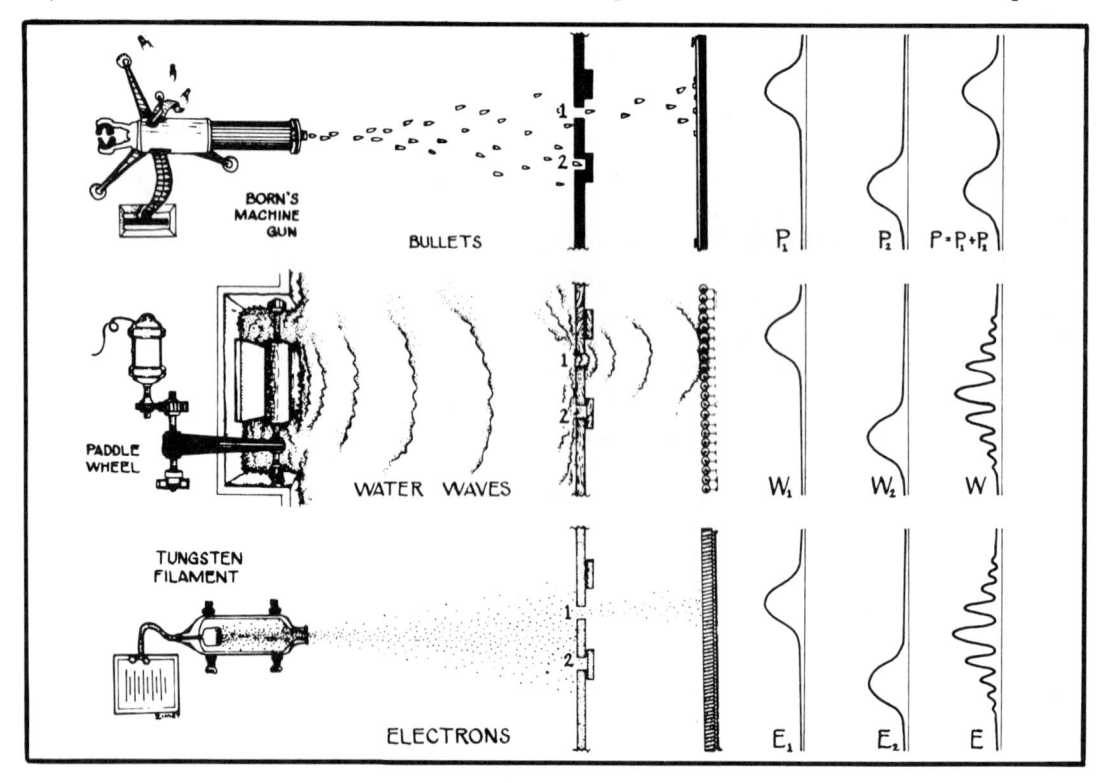

the bullets hit when they went through the slits. He shot bullets first through one slit, then through the other, and then through both at once. He made curve diagrams showing the places where the bullets had hit the screen when one door or both were open. The largest number of bullets hit the screen directly behind the opening: 1 slit , the second slit , and both slits . Bullets are like particles and make the pattern one would expect.

In the second room Born set up a paddle wheel to send water through the slits. He conducted the experiment in the same way, sending water first through one slit, then the other, and then through both at once. Again he recorded the pattern the waves made on the screen. The pattern when both slits were open showed the expected pattern for water waves that were affected by two sources of water. The patterns appeared , , .

In the third room he set up an apparatus to send electrons through the slits in the same way he had sent bullets and water. Since electrons are particles, the logical expectation is that they would form a pattern like the bullet pattern. The electrons behaved like particles, like the bullets, going through the slits, but they made a pattern on the screen like the water waves. The switch from particle pattern to wave pattern made no sense.

Born shone a light behind the slits to see what was going on. When he watched the electron particles with his light, they made a particle pattern like bullets instead of the wave pattern they made when he was not watching. Then he dimmed the light and the pattern began to look like the wave patterns again. His conclusion was that electrons are one way *or* the other. If anyone sees them they are particles; if no one sees them they are waves. Electrons seem to come into existence as real objects or particles only when someone observes them. Timothy Ferris said in *Coming of Age in the Milky Way*, "they are participants in an act of creation."

Another strange feature of atomic particles is called

"Physicists strive for completeness, because they know a great theory cannot be a partial picture of nature but must give the complete laws of a class of events."

Heinz Pagels, *The Cosmic Code*

"Laws of nature are merely hypotheses devised to explain that ever-shifting phantasmagoria of thought which we dignify with high-sounding names of the world and the universe."

Theodore H. Gaster, *The New Golden Bough*

quantum mechanical tunneling through the barrier. It works like this. An electron, or any atomic particle, locked in a container with no way to get out *can* appear outside the container. Scientists explain this strange behavior with probability waves. The wave equation shows that an electron in a cup has a probability of appearing outside the cup—like stepping or tunneling through the wall of the cup. No one sees this happen; mathematical equations prove that it does. Transistors, many electronic instruments, even digital watches have parts whose electronic signals are amplified (made larger) by quantum tunneling effect. These are electrons acting like waves.

These discoveries ended determinism (the idea that events are governed by nature's laws) and classical objectivity (events occur independent of human observation). Quantum particles do not follow predictable laws of nature or exist objectively. Human observation determines their form; that is, they change when a human is present and observes them. Quantum reality required new thinking; it is an observer-created reality.

The Challenge of Disorder

For centuries, humans have sought order to give them more control over their lives and, consequently, more security and comfort. These discoveries concerning atoms, the basic building blocks in the universe, were leading to disorder, it seemed, not order.

How could scientists measure a thing that pops

Left: Transistors, such as the ones that make this cassette player operate, are based in part on the atom's tunneling effect. Right: An atomic particle can "tunnel" through "solid" matter by traveling through the space within the atomic shells.

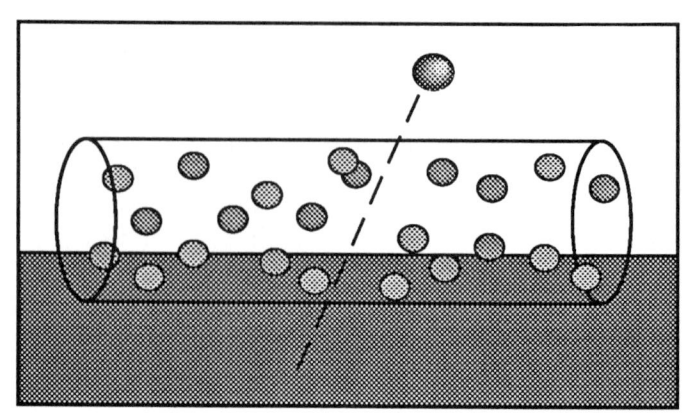

from one orbit to another, speeds up and slows down, weaves its way through other atoms, shifts from particle to wave to particle, and tunnels through walls? Since quantum behavior is random, scientists used the same procedures mathematicians used to establish probability tables for throwing dice. They first charted the possibilities and then established the mathematical probabilities for any possible outcome to occur. Werner Heisenberg, Niels Bohr, Erwin Schrödinger, and Paul Dirac worked on this problem.

In 1926, German scientist Werner Heisenberg set out to predict the future position and velocity of a particle. He ended up inventing the *uncertainty principle*. The uncertainty principle says that accurate measurements are impossible because a particle or wave changes according to the person and the way he or she is measuring. But, it says, it is possible to predict a certain range of measurements.

At the same time Heisenberg developed the uncertainty principle, Bohr developed the *complementary principle*. The complementary principle is the theory that an electron must have two measurements, one for its particle nature and one for its wave nature, and together the two measurements describe the electron. One measurement complements, or completes, the other, he stated.

An Austrian-German physicist, Erwin Schrödinger, developed a theory of wave mechanics (the workings of the atom as a wave). This theory formulated an equation showing the numerical probability of finding an electron in orbit. He based this theory on de Broglie's idea that an electron has a wave to guide its travels. If an electron's position is plotted repeatedly, and each place it appears is represented by a dot, a pattern emerges, showing the places where it appears most often and where it seldom appears. From such a pattern of positions, Schrödinger's equation calculates the probability for the electron's appearance at a given place.

Schrödinger did for an electron's wave function what Heisenberg did for an electron's particle function. Since electron behavior is random, its position at

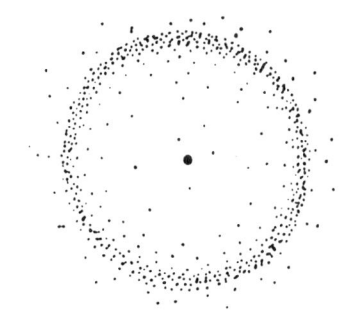

Erwin Schrödinger (top) figured out a way to predict the probability of an electron's location (bottom).

a particular time is impossible to predict; only its probability, its likelihood, of being in a certain position at a certain time is possible to predict.

Paul Dirac was a mathematician who held the same position at Cambridge University in England that Newton had held three centuries earlier. It was Dirac who developed a theory to show that Heisenberg's particle measurements and Schrödinger's wave measurements are equivalent: The two measurements use different symbols and numbers to describe the same thing. Dirac's theory shows how to transform or change one measurement into the other so that there is one answer instead of two.

In *The Cosmic Code*, Heinz Pagels said of this long, step-by-step process: "The complex theory, including Dirac's transformation theory, finally became called quantum mechanics or quantum theory, a new mathematically consistent dynamics which replaced classical physics. The labor of nearly three decades had yielded a new world dynamics."

Quantum Theory Creates New Mysteries

In the first thirty years of the twentieth century, scientists made great progress toward an understanding of the design of the atom's universe. Quantum theory developed in steps from Max Planck's quanta and constant h to Paul Dirac's transformation theory. But the path to development puzzled scientists as they saw nature behave in ways they never expected. Even though much progress had been made, scientists felt compelled to search further for answers to the

Left: The Bohr model of an atom. Center: De Broglie's wave mechanics. Right: Schrödinger's mathematical probability electron theory. Mathematician Paul Dirac figured out that de Broglie's and Schrödinger's theories were two different ways of showing the same thing.

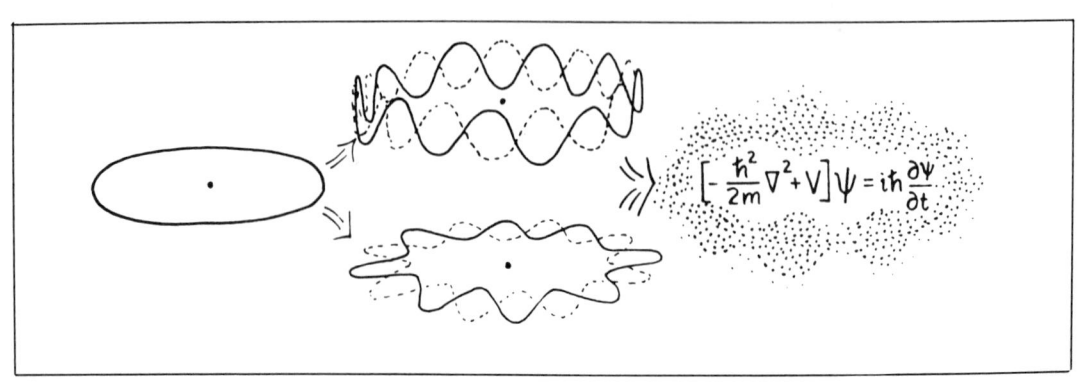

mystery. Quantum theory is a useful theory, but at the time Dirac came up with his transformation theory, much of the atom's mystery was yet to be solved.

Scientists used quantum theory to study nuclear physics, the science concerned with the atom's nucleus. Engineers used quantum theory to develop technology for transistors, computers, and lasers. Chemists and biologists used it to make new discoveries in their fields. Physicists and astronomers used it to explore astrophysics, the combination of astronomy and physics. Quantum theory may have solved one mystery, but it opened the door to many new mysteries.

Furthermore, the randomness of the atom and the dependence on probability rather than prediction left many scientists uneasy. Quantum mechanics is unsettling because it describes a universe with no more order than a coin toss or a dice throw.

Einstein never accepted quantum theory. He spent the last half of his life searching for a unified theory that would predict the behavior of the atom, but he died without finding one. Even on the night he died in 1955, he left papers beside his bed with equations he had worked on during the day. He objected to the randomness of the quantum theory, the lack of nature's objectivity and predictability.

In a letter to Niels Bohr, he wrote at one point in the quantum search: "I find the idea quite intolerable that an electron exposed to radiation [the emission of energy] should chose *of its own free will*, not only its moment to jump off, but also its direction. In that case, I would rather be a cobbler [shoemaker], or even an employee in a gaming-house, than a physicist."

At another time, he told Max Born: "Quantum mechanics is certainly imposing...but an inner voice tells me that it is not yet the real thing. The theory says a lot, but does not really bring us any closer to the secret of the 'old one' [God]. I, at any rate, am convinced that *He* is not playing dice."

New Tools for Exploring the Universe

The search for order in the universe began with primitive people and their magic. After thousands of

"I am quite convinced that someone will eventually come up with a theory whose objects, connected by laws, are not probabilities but considered facts."

Albert Einstein

"While today it is conceivable that physics will realize its dream [of a unified theory]..., I doubt it."

Heinz Pagels, *The Cosmic Code*

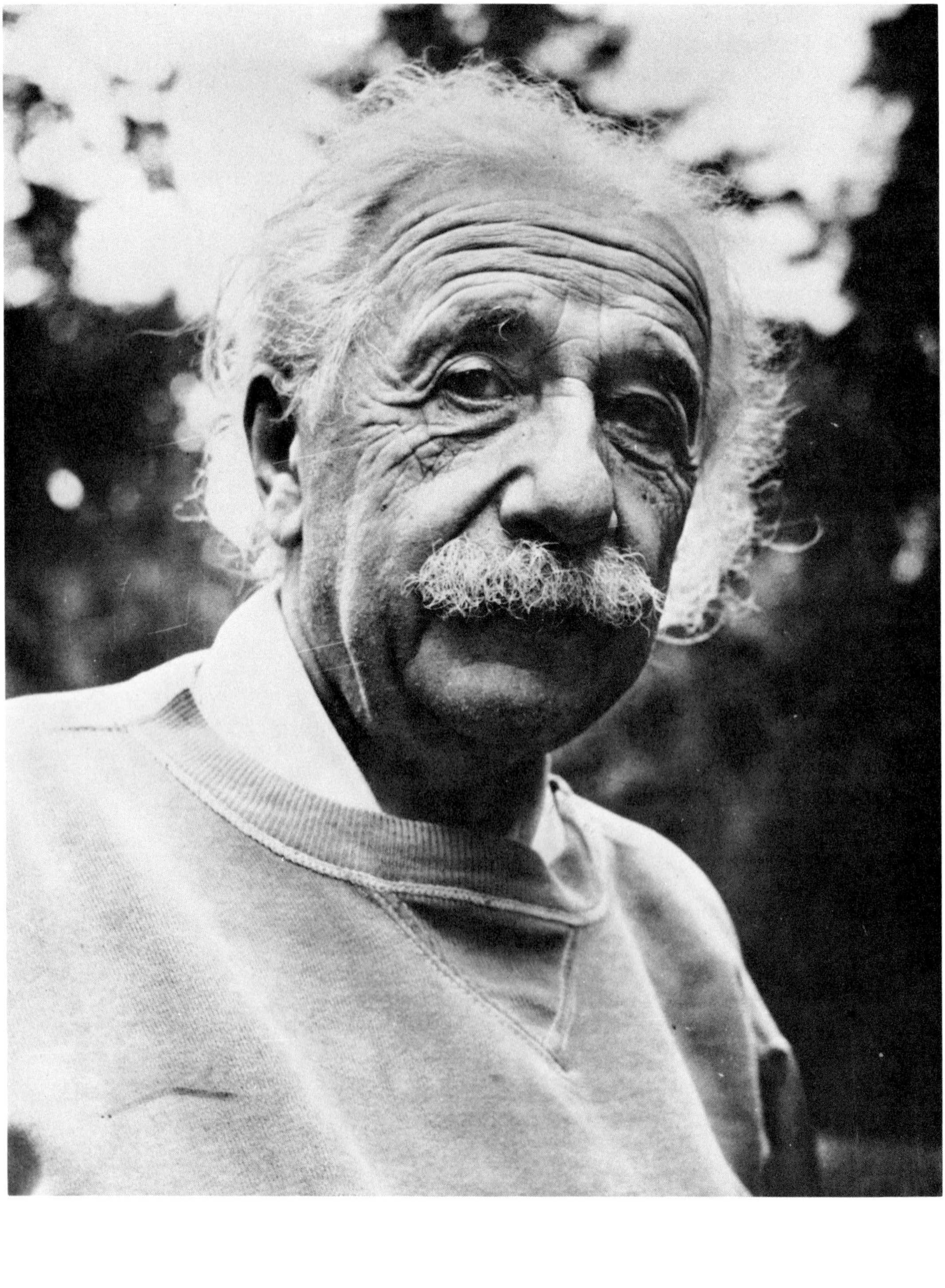

years of searching for order, do we conclude that our universe is random, no more orderly than a coin toss?

In *The Cosmic Code*, Heinz Pagels expresses views different from Einstein's. He writes, "Quantum randomness cannot be beat; the God that plays dice is an honest gambler.... The house of a God that plays dice has many rooms. We can live in only one room at a time, but it is the whole house that is reality." Pagels emphasizes that quantum randomness is foolproof; there are no stacked decks or loaded dice. At least the game is honest. Furthermore, atom randomness is only part of the universe. Reality is the whole design of the universe, not one part of it, Pagels reminds us.

The whole design of the universe, as it is described during any era, is dependent on the amount of knowledge available at the time. The development of quantum theory provided new knowledge about the atom that yielded two results. First, the knowledge strengthened and complicated the concept of relativity, the interdependence of events, their measurements, and the mind's perceptions about them. Second, the knowledge gave scientists tools for further study of the universe—from its tiniest bits to its farthest reaches, its origin to its end—and an opportunity to describe yet a more complex and more thorough design.

Albert Einstein changed forever the way scientists look at the design of the universe.

Five

The Beginning and the End

By the 1930s, one-third of the way through the twentieth century, scientists had major new discoveries to use: Einstein's Special and General Relativity and the quantum theory of the atom. These theories served as important tools for scientists to make further discoveries about the mystery of the universe.

Both Einstein's theory and atomic theory use the idea of relativity, the idea that one thing is relative to, connected to, or dependent on another. In Special Relativity, time is relative to space; in $E = mc^2$, energy is relative to mass; in General Relativity, gravitational force is relative to matter, energy, motion, time, space, and mass. In quantum theory, measurements of proton waves are relative to measurements of proton particles. The mystery of relativity had become an important idea in the search for order in the universe.

After 1930, scientists used these findings to expand the limits of knowledge about the universe. Some scientists used quantum, or atomic, theory to continue to search for the tiniest bit that makes up all things. They studied the nucleus of the atom and became known as nuclear physicists. Other scientists used Einstein's theories to study distant stars and outer space. They became known as astrophysicists because they combined astronomy, the study of the stars, with

Opposite: Some scientists used Einstein's theories and the other new ideas that came from them to explore the beginning and end of the universe.

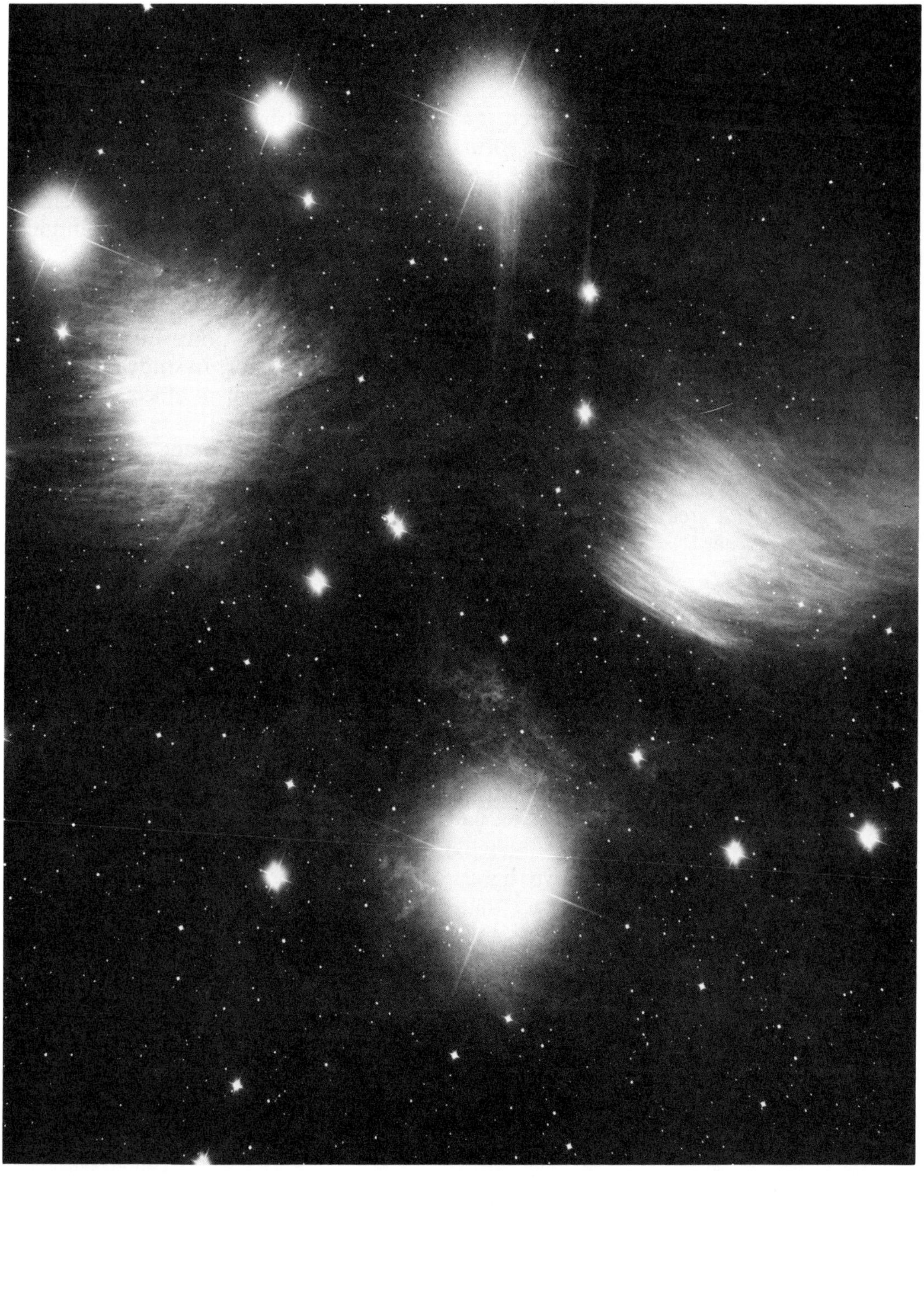

> "According to determinism, the universe may be viewed as a great clockwork set in motion by a divine hand at the beginning of time and then left unattended."
>
> Heinz Pagels, *The Cosmic Code*

> "Today there is a wide measure of agreement... that the stream of knowledge is heading towards a non-mechanical reality; the universe begins to look more like a great thought than a great machine."
>
> Physicist James Jeans

physics.

Other scientists combined the knowledge acquired by nuclear physicists with the knowledge acquired by astrophysicists. They used this combined knowledge to search for answers to even bigger mysteries. How do stars form and die? How did the universe begin? How might it end?

In order to do these complex new studies, scientists needed elaborate equipment developed from modern technology. Nuclear physicists needed huge accelerators and colliders to smash the atom's nucleus, and atomic reactors to control nuclear chain reaction. Astrophysicists needed more powerful telescopes, spectroscopes, and wave detectors to study stars in distant space. Each kind of equipment aided scientists in a different phase of their search.

After 1930, nuclear physicists made several important discoveries about the atom. They discovered *fission*, the separation of a nucleus and the formation of new atoms. They discovered *fusion*, the combining of nuclei into a new atom. They discovered that matter has an opposite—*antimatter*. They discovered many new matter and force particles which they named and grouped into categories. These discoveries were made in the search for the tiniest particle in the universe. But the discoveries also helped scientists answer other questions about the universe. Let us look at each of these discoveries about the atom's nucleus and at the way scientists made the discoveries.

Fission and Fusion

In fission, an unstable heavy atom separates into two lighter atoms. Uranium^{235} is a heavy, unstable atom that can be separated. When a neutron bombards a uranium^{235} atom, the uranium nucleus absorbs the neutron. It elongates (stretches out) and then separates into two lighter atoms. This fission process may produce different combinations of smaller nuclei, or new atoms. In an everyday example, the process would be like sending a grape seed to bombard a peach and having the peach separate into two plums. In another fission process, a neutron bombards the nucleus, releases an energy particle, and the result is one new atom with a different nucleus.

Separating a uranium atom releases about two hundred million electron volts of energy. By comparison, a molecule of dynamite, or TNT, releases thirty electron volts of energy. When an abundance of uranium^{235} atoms exist together, the neutrons set free by the separation bombard other uranium nuclei and cause them to separate, releasing other neutrons. This process is called a *chain reaction*. Scientists use an atomic reactor, a device that controls the speed and number of neutrons that bombard uranium^{235} atoms, to prevent runaway chain reactions. Fission was used in the atomic bomb that the American military dropped on Hiroshima, Japan, during World War II. Fission is the process that makes power in nuclear power plants.

In fusion, two light atoms fuse into one heavier atom. This process takes place in two ways. In the laboratory, fusion takes place at very high speeds. In nature, fusion takes place at very high temperatures, called *nuclear burning*. Fusion takes place most readily by fusing two hydrogen atoms, the lightest atom, into one helium atom, the second lightest atom. Other light atoms fuse into heavier atoms such as carbon, oxygen, or nickel, but only at much higher temperatures or speeds. In an everyday example, fusion is like speeding two grapes in an accelerator until they fuse into a plum.

Like fission, fusion releases energy. Accelerating two hydrogen atoms to speeds near the speed of light fuses them into a helium atom and releases 26,700,000 electron volts of energy. Fusion is the process that

In the process of fission (left), a heavy atom is split into lighter atoms, creating powerful new energy. In fusion (right), lighter atoms are combined, or fused, into new heavier atoms, again creating powerful new energy.

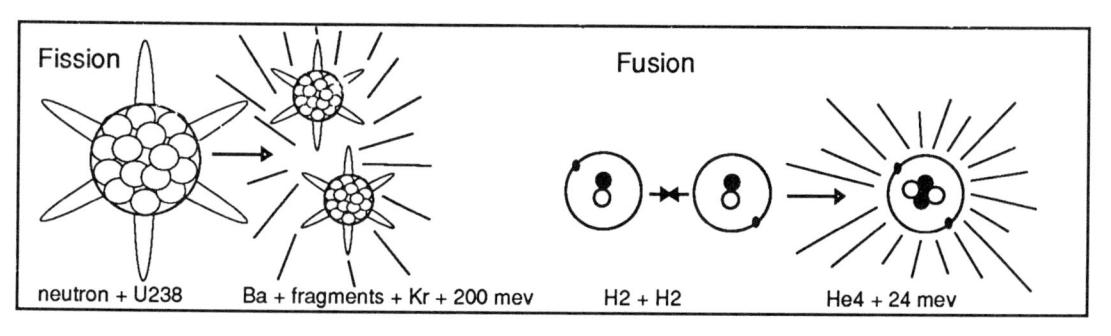

Fission		Fusion	
neutron + U238	Ba + fragments + Kr + 200 mev	H2 + H2	He4 + 24 mev

Atomic theories are tested in accelerators and colliders. In these gigantic machines (Fermilab in Illinois has an accelerator three miles in diameter), particles of atoms are accelerated to nearly the speed of light and then slammed into a target. In the top diagram below, protons are accelerated and then slammed into an outside target. In the bottom diagram, protons are accelerated in one direction, antiprotons in the other. The two kinds of particles are then slammed into each other.

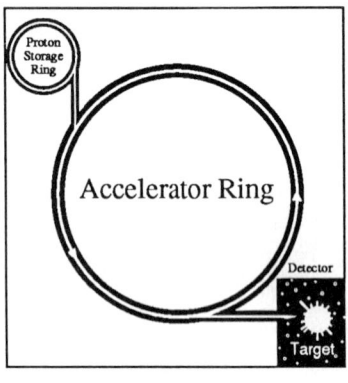

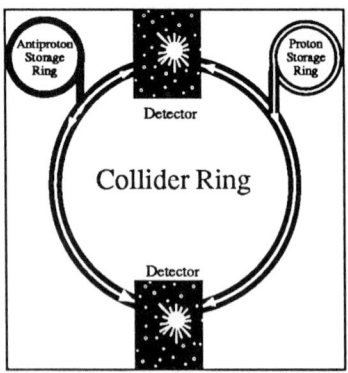

makes the sun shine. Our sun fuses 657 million tons of hydrogen into 653 million tons of helium every second. The missing four million tons discharge as energy, the energy we feel as the sun's warmth. Scientists estimate that the sun has been burning, or fusing hydrogen into helium, for approximately five billion years and will continue the process for another five billion years. Knowledge of fusion not only helped scientists understand our sun, it also helped them understand the process by which stars form and die.

Experimenting with Accelerators and Colliders

For scientists to conduct fusion experiments in the laboratory, as well as other experiments involving the atom's nucleus, they needed powerful machines—particle accelerators and particle colliders. Accelerators accelerate protons to near the speed of light and smash them against a wall. Colliders accelerate one group of protons in one direction and another group in the opposite direction and then smash them into each other.

To conduct an experiment, a researcher most often uses hydrogen atoms since they are abundant and simple—the hydrogen nucleus has only one proton. A computer releases a number of atoms into the first chamber of an accelerator or a collider. There the protons are removed. The protons are sent down a long curved tube, about an inch across and several miles long. Electromagnets send pulses of electromagnetic energy through the tube until the protons move at 90 percent, or higher, of the speed of light. Magnets gather the particles into a thin beam. When they are going fast enough, they are rerouted and smashed into a target or into each other. Detectors, hooked up to computers, record the results before the particles combine again. Other records come from photos of the particles' high-speed flights and their collisions and explosions. From these records physicists can identify known particles, verify theories, and find new particles.

Today, there are many accelerators. Stanford University in California has one that is two miles long. Fermilab in Illinois has a longer one, as does CERN (European Center for Nuclear Research) in Geneva,

Fermilab in Batavia, Illinois. The largest circle is the main accelerator.

Switzerland. CERN also built another massive machine, a collider with a circumference of seventeen miles! Fritjof Capra, a researcher in high-energy physics, pointed out the irony that experiments on the tiniest bits of matter require the most gigantic equipment.

Antimatter

In the process of working with mathematical equations and experimenting with accelerators and colliders, physicists developed the theory of antimatter. This is the theory that every particle of matter has an equal companion, equal except that is has the opposite electrical charge. For example, if protons with positive charges exist, there must be protons with negative charges. Physicists named these *antiprotons*. If electrons with negative charges exist, there must be electrons with positive charges. Physicists named these *positrons*. The theory of antimatter changed physicists' way of thinking by allowing them to think of all particles in pairs.

The theory of antimatter was first predicted by Paul Dirac's transformation theory (discussed in chapter 4). Antielectrons, or positrons, were discovered in 1932 by Carl Anderson. Before the end of the 1930s, Dirac and Anderson had won the Nobel Prize for their discovery of antimatter.

Matter and antimatter cannot exist together,

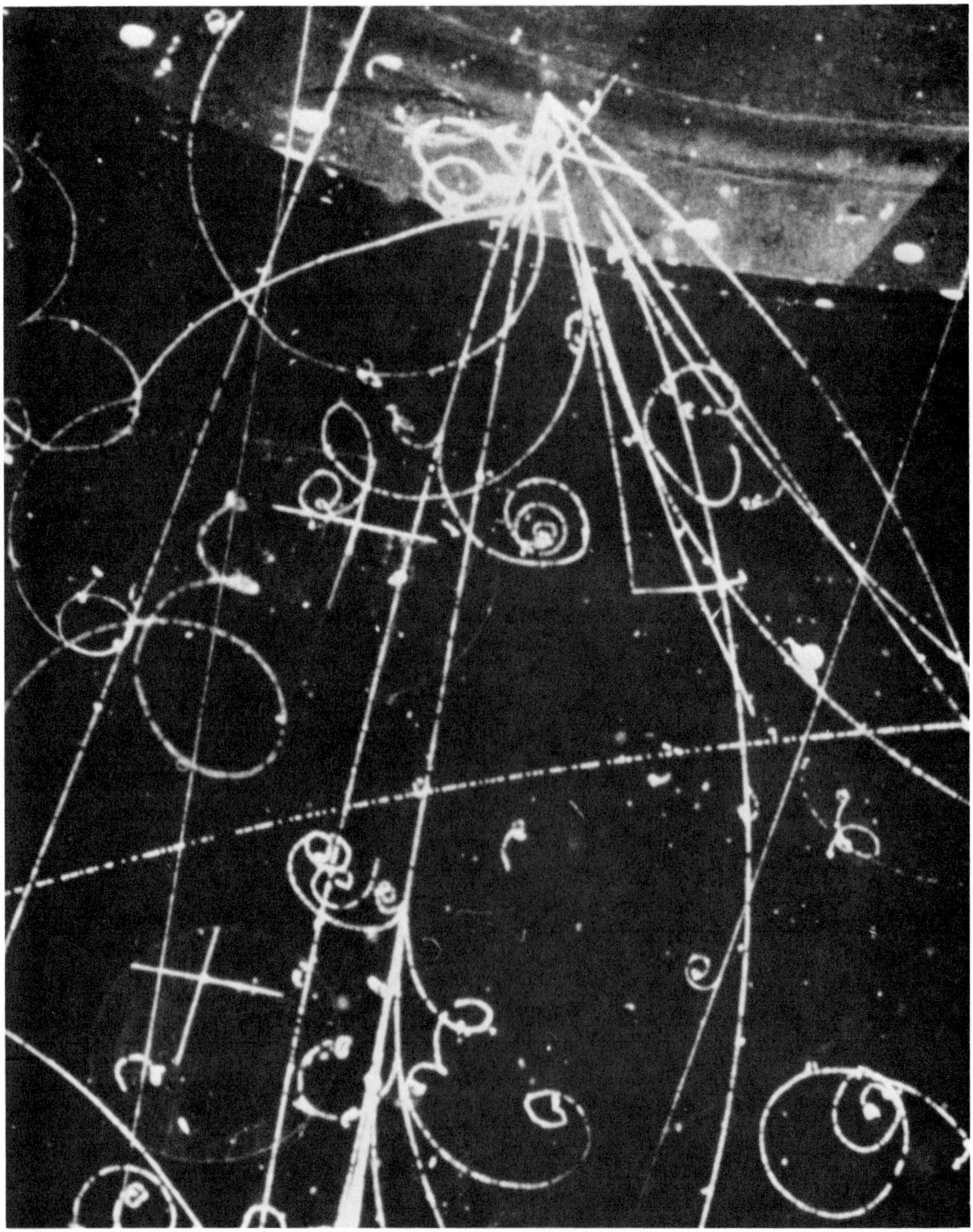

because opposite charges attract. If they do come together, they collide, explode, and destroy each other. In an everyday example, if a tennis player put an anti-tennis ball into her pocket that already held a tennis ball, both would explode. If a baseball player got tagged out at second base by an anti-baseball player, both would disappear in an explosion. The theory of antimatter provides yet another perspective on the way one thing is related to, or connected to, another.

The discovery of antimatter was important. Physicists eventually made and stored antiprotons which they could use in a collider to bombard protons. The resulting explosions produced forces that shattered the nucleus of the atom and made it possible to discover new and smaller particles in their search for the tiniest bit of matter in the universe. Also, the discovery helped later scientists develop theories about what happened at the beginning of the universe.

Classifying Tiny Particles

Accelerating and colliding protons helped scientists identify many new particles in the subatomic universe. These particles are a part of the universe that had never been known before. Many of them have only short life spans before they combine with other particles, but in new experiments they appear again. Scientists had to classify these particles and give them names so that they could make order in this tiny universe.

Scientists developed levels of classifications. First, they put all matter particles in one category and all force particles into another. Then, they went on to make subcategories for the two major groups. As they classified the particles, they made up names for both the categories and the particles.

Stephen Hawking explained the naming of the two major categories, matter and force. He said that all known particles in the universe can be divided into two categories: those with spin 1/2 (matter particles) and those with spin 0, 1, 2 (force particles). The word "spin" does not refer to the way the particles behave; it refers to the way a particle must be turned before it "looks" the same again, in a mathematical way, to an experimenter. Matter particles with spin 1/2 (electrons,

Opposite: This shows a pattern which occurs when subatomic particles hit their target in an accelerator.

This diagram illustrates spin theory as it relates to force particles.

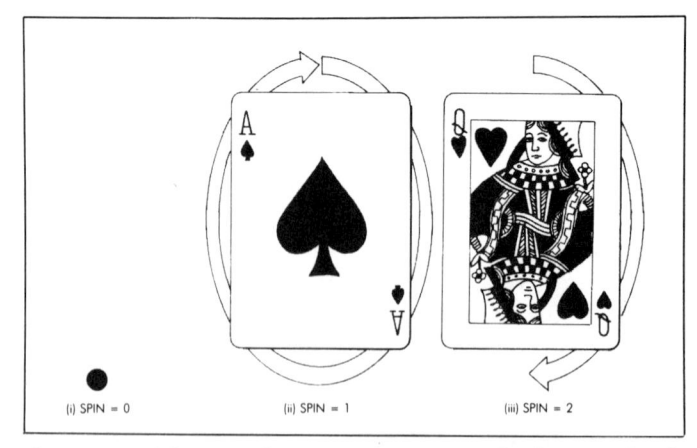

(i) SPIN = 0   (ii) SPIN = 1   (iii) SPIN = 2

for example) must be turned two revolutions to look the same, first one (1/) and then a second (/2).

Force particles, the particles that exist between matter particles, come in three varieties or spins. Like matter particles, they are numbered according to the spins necessary to make them "look" the same again mathematically. A spin 0 particle requires no spins because, like a dot, it looks the same from all angles. A spin 1 particle requires one complete revolution to look the same. A spin 2 particle requires only half a turn because one half is a mirror image of the other.

Spin theory, developed originally by Paul Dirac during the 1920s and 1930s, gave physicists a better understanding of the fundamental particles and forces. As new particles were found, the categories had to be further subdivided, a task done by Enrico Fermi and Satyendra Nath Bose.

Italian physicist Enrico Fermi further classified all matter particles that had spin 1/2. These are the particles within protons, electrons, and neutrons. Indian physicist Satyendra Nath Bose further classified all force particles that had spins 0, 1, and 2. Most of these force particles live a short time only, but they reappear. In the process of classifying particles, physicists also gave the particles names. Fermi and Bose used their last names for categories: fermions and bosons. Many names appear on the particle charts; hadrons, leptons, muons, and neutrinos are only a sampling of them. When Fermi saw how many particles there were, he joked that had he known the complicated "outcome of nuclear physics, he would have studied zoology."

The Tiniest Building Blocks

Nuclear physicists now think they have found what they have been searching for—the tiniest building blocks in the universe and the fundamental forces that hold them together. Most physicists think *quarks* are the tiniest bits in the universe, even tinier than the subparticles on Fermi's charts. They were named "quarks" by Murray Gell-Mann, a physicist from California who worked on the discovery. The name, which is a German word for a curd of cheese, comes from a line in James Joyce's novel, *Ulysses:* "Three quarks for Muster Mark." Physicists have found six kinds of quarks. None of the names mean anything; they are simply labels. The six kinds are called *up, down, strange, charmed, bottom,* and *top.* The three varieties of each kind of quark are identified as *red, blue,* and *yellow.* For example, according to one model, a proton has two up quarks and one down quark. A neutron has two down quarks and one up quark.

Stephen Hawking believes it may be possible to find still smaller particles, but, he says, "We do have some theoretical reasons for believing that we have, or are very near to, a knowledge of the ultimate building blocks of nature."

Nuclear physicists also think they have found the fundamental forces that hold the building blocks together. They have identified four forces: gravitational force, electromagnetic force, weak nuclear force, and strong nuclear force. Now physicists want to find a single theory that will explain all four forces. So far they have found theories to unify three of them, but they have found no way yet to unify gravitational force into the theory. A unified theory of forces is a mystery still to be solved.

The Drive for Beauty

Nuclear physicists have taken us a long way toward an understanding of the smallest part of nature, but

"Absolute space, in its own nature, without relation to anything external, remains always similar and immovable."

Sir Isaac Newton

"Einstein had replaced Newton's absolute space with a network of light beams; [the grid of light beams] was the absolute grid, within which space itself becomes supple."

Timothy Ferris, *Coming of Age in the Milky Way*

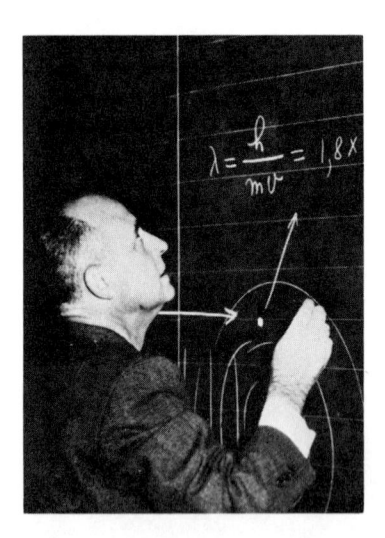

Certain subatomic particles (parts of atoms) are named after the scientists who worked on theories relating to them. Fermions are named after physicist Enrico Fermi (above).

the mystery of the atom is not completely solved. The discoveries of fission and fusion, antimatter and particle spin, quarks, and forces represent steps in the search and indicate the limits of what we know about the smallest bit in the universe. Leon Lederman, the director of the Fermilab particle accelerator in Illinois, had this to say about the state of quantum mechanics: "The trouble we're in now is that the standard model [of quantum theory] is very elegant, it's very powerful, it explains so much—but it's not complete....It's too complicated....The picture is not beautiful, and that drive for beauty and simplicity and symmetry has been an unfailing guidepost to how to go in physics."

Leon Lederman's remarks seem to suggest that physicists must pursue this search for simpler order, but scholars who view the achievements of nuclear physics in the context of society at large are less certain. Science historian Gerald Holt, for one, questions whether the quality of life on earth has been improved by the development of scientific technology. In his book, *The Advancement of Science, and Its Burdens*, Holt points out the decreased costs and the greater availability of energy, food, information, and medicine to large numbers of people. But he also points out that "The gifts of high technology, from computers to nuclear reactors [have] become in many quarters the very symbol of technological changes undermining societal objectives, the gift that is a Trojan horse." The gift of scientific advancement, he says, has brought destruction.

Others believe it is unfair to blame science for the misuse of scientific discoveries. In his book, *Advice to a Young Scientist*, Sir Peter Medawar says, "The direction of scientific endeavor is determined by political decisions as...acts of judgment that lie outside science itself." In other words, scientists discover objective knowledge; politicians decide the right use for it. Medawar's statement reminds us how important relativity is in the twentieth century. Not only are findings within science connected and dependent on one another, but the whole field of science is connected to other fields, like politics, ethics, and sociology.

The technology of science has become extremely complex. For example, this is one part of the control room at the Stanford Linear Accelerator. Some scientists ask whether all of this advancement is a good thing.

A Larger View of the Universe

Let us turn attention now from discoveries about the smallest bits in the universe to stars and outer space, the largest part of nature. How have scientists used the tools of Einstein's theory to solve new space mysteries?

In order to study objects in outer space, astronomers needed better measuring tools. New technological instruments have allowed scientists to measure both the location and composition of stars more accurately. Technologists have continued to make more powerful telescopes since Galileo's time. In the late 1850s physicists Gustav Kirchhoff and Robert Bunsen developed a *spectroscope.* This instrument marks off the color spectrum in lines. The lines represent atomic elements, like hydrogen, helium, and iron. With this instrument scientists could discover what stars are made of. An American, George Ellery Hale, invented a *spectrohelioscope,* a more accurate instrument that measures the spectrum one wavelength at a time. A *wave detector*, which measures waves too weak to show any light or color, uses a conversion method that measures temperature. These instruments measure the location of stars and their distance from us.

These instruments, along with the discovery of something called the *Doppler effect,* or *red shift*, allowed scientists to solve several mysteries about outer space. In 1842, Austrian physicist Christian Johann Doppler found that light from a source moving away

As scientists try to get more information about the outer reaches of the universe, their instruments become more and more sophisticated. No longer is the telescope of Galileo sufficient.

from the viewer appears as red colors and light from a source moving toward the viewer appears as blue colors. Blue and red are at opposite ends of the spectrum. Then in 1929, American astronomer Edwin Hubble made a revolutionary discovery about the stars: He discovered a pattern of shifts toward red colors. This meant that the stars are moving away from us and the universe is expanding. In *The Tao of Physics*, Fritjof Capra explains that distant stars move away faster than nearer stars, "nearby galaxies at several thousand miles per second, farther ones at higher speeds, and the farthest at velocities approaching the speed of light." Hubble's discovery of red shifts means that the universe has been expanding and evolving since the beginning of time and will continue to do so. The idea of an evolving universe opens up new questions about its beginning and end.

The Distance of Stars

With new and refined instruments and with new theories available to them, scientists have acquired knowledge that helps them solve new mysteries about stars: How many stars are there? How far away are they? In order to measure the vast distances in space, scientists use the measurement of *light years*. Light travels at 186,000 miles per second. One light year is the distance light travels in a year, about six trillion miles.

In light years, our sun is eight minutes away. The star nearest earth is four light years away. The spiral disk that is our galaxy, the Milky Way, is 100,000 light years across. Our sun is an average-size yellow star near the inner edge of one of the spirals. The Milky Way is one of several hundred thousand million galaxies, and each galaxy has some hundred thousand million stars in it. It is no wonder that when he looked through his telescope Galileo said, "the number of small ones is quite beyond calculation."

The Andromeda galaxy is two million light years away. Beyond Andromeda lies the Virgo Supercluster some sixty million light years away. And numerous galaxies lie beyond Virgo. Quasars, the farthest known stars, are thought to be stars in young galaxies; they are a billion light years away. We have come a long way from thinking of the sky as "a low tent roof."

Finding stars at such great distances, scientists developed the idea of *lookback time*. We cannot see a star until its light reaches us. And stars are so far away, requiring such a long time for their light to travel, that we see them today as they appeared in the past. For example, we see stars in the Coma cluster as they existed seven hundred million (700,000,000) years ago. Since quasars are farther away, their lookback time is even longer.

Above: Christian Johann Doppler discovered *red shift*, now called the Doppler effect: Light from sources moving away from the viewer appears red; light from sources coming toward the viewer appears blue. Below: Edwin Hubble discovered a trend in the cosmos to red light, meaning the universe appears to be expanding.

> "Herman Bondi and Thomas Gold promulgated in 1948 what they called the steady state model. According to their theory, the universe was infinitely old and generally unchanging: There had been no creation event, no high-density infancy from which the universe has evolved."
>
> Timothy Ferris, *Coming of Age in the Milky Way*

> "The discovery that the universe is expanding was one of the great revolutions of the twentieth century."
>
> Stephen Hawking, *A Brief History of Time*

The Life of Stars

In addition to providing information about numbers and locations of stars, the new instruments and theories have made it possible for scientists to discover what stars are made of and how they begin and end. A star forms from hydrogen atoms and dust, a mixture that contracts, and eventually the atoms in the mixture fuse into new atoms.

In the first stage, hydrogen atoms, mixed with dust, float freely. The gravity of these gaseous particles cause the mass to contract and become increasingly more dense. As the mass continues to contract, the temperature rises under the increased pressure. When the temperature reaches ten million degrees, the hydrogen atoms contract with so much pressure and motion that hydrogen protons fuse and form helium atoms. This fusion, which is nuclear burning, emits enormous amounts of energy and causes the star to shine. But the mass also creates a gravitational field around it which exerts pressure inward. The balance of energy fields—energy emitted outward from within, gravitational force pressing inward from without—is a star that can remain stable for a long time. Eventually, however, the hydrogen fuel gets used up and the star begins to die.

Star Deaths

Stars come to their end in several ways, depending on their size. The different ways of ending have different names: supernovas, red giants, black and white dwarfs, and black holes.

A *supernova* is the end of the biggest stars. These stars have the shortest life span because their huge size must burn hotter and faster in order to counteract their gravitational force. Thus they burn their hydrogen into helium faster. Then the helium atoms fuse into heavier atoms, like carbon and oxygen, causing even greater heat and faster burning of the atomic fuel. When no fuel is left, the remaining matter rushes inward, a process called imploding, the opposite of exploding. The mounting heat and pressure from the implosion cause the mass to explode. The explosion is seen as a supernova. Only a dense spinning core remains.

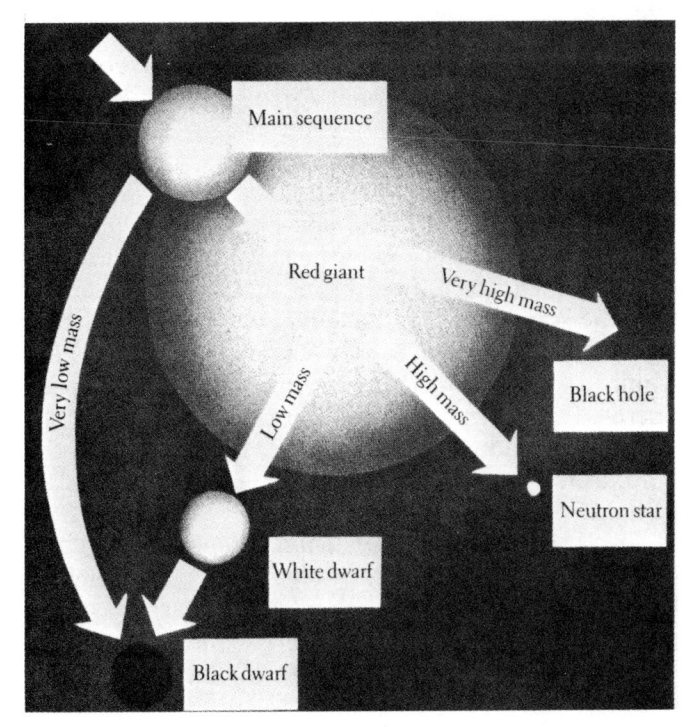

This diagram shows the stages in the lives and deaths of stars. A typical star first becomes a red giant like our sun. Eventually, if it has low mass, it will fade away to a white dwarf and finally a black dwarf. If it has high mass, it will become an ultracompact neutron star, or possibly a black hole.

Red giants and the dwarfs have less dramatic endings. When an average-size star like our sun has fused all the hydrogen in the core to helium, the star contracts and the temperature rises. The added heat ignites the remaining hydrogen outside the core and the star expands, becoming a red giant, a star about to go out. After all available nuclear fuel is used up, the mass cools and contracts. Our sun will become a red giant in approximately five billion years. It is about halfway through its lifetime.

White dwarfs are small stars about to die. When their fuel is burned up, they are too small to implode and explode like a supernova or to swell like a red giant. They just shrink. What is left blazes white hot and is called a white dwarf. As it cools, it turns to yellow and then to red. Eventually, it cools to a black lump and becomes a black dwarf.

A *black hole* is an even more dramatic way for a star to end than a supernova. When stars with three to five times the mass of our sun burn up all their fuel,

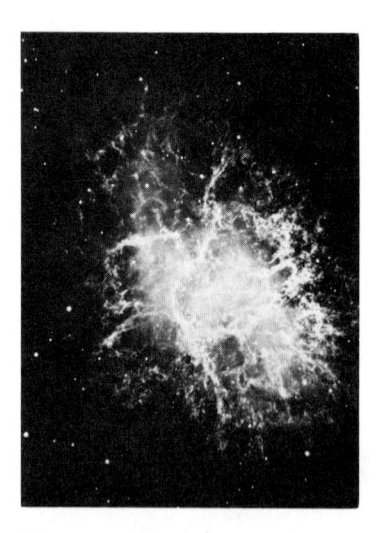

The remains of a supernova.

they implode, but they do not explode. The energy created by the contracting mass is too weak to counteract the greater gravitational force of the huge mass pressing inward. The mass contracts for a while, but when it implodes, the great mass creates such a strong gravitational field that space-time curves so far that it folds in upon itself. When space-time folds in upon itself, nothing, not even light, can escape. Light bends within curved space-time. From outside the collapsed star, the star appears to have no light and looks like a black hole. In an everyday example, a black hole would be like a round light bulb suspended in space operated by a remote-control dimmer switch. The bulb would dim gradually, but when the light went out, the bulb, as if by magic, would disappear with the last ray of light.

In *A Brief History of Time*, Stephen Hawking, who has done much study of black holes, calls a black hole a *singularity*. He defines a singularity as "[a] point in space-time at which space-time curvature becomes infinite," continuing without end until it is nothing. That curvature becomes infinite at a point when the collapsed star's gravitational field becomes so strong that space-time bends around the mass in tighter and tighter curves. According to the Theory of Relativity, time and space have different measurements from the frame of reference inside the black hole and from a frame of reference outside the black hole. Inside the black hole, the mass continues to contract into a denser, smaller ball. Because space-time turns in tighter and tighter curves, nothing escapes, neither light nor a ray that has energy to send a message. From a frame of reference outside the star, the wave signals slow down as the mass contracts and space-time curves. Someone in a spaceship timing signals from the star would observe longer and longer intervals between signals. After the point of singularity, there would be no more signals; time would have stopped, would have become infinite. After the point of singularity, no light would escape and the star would appear to have no space, leaving only a black hole.

Knowledge about the life cycle of a star illustrates how one branch of science depends on another. Nuclear physics provided information about atoms and fusion; astronomy identified the different kinds of stars. By connecting the information from the two branches of science, we learn how stars are born and die and see how the mystery of relativity works in yet another way.

The Big Bang

Out of all the knowledge scientists have acquired in the twentieth century, from Relativity Theory, quantum theory, nuclear physics, and astrophysics, they have developed the big bang theory to explain the beginning of the universe. The big bang theory is that the universe developed from a gigantic explosion at a point in time. Since then everything in the universe has been expanding from the point and moment of that explosion and is still expanding. Space and time began with the big bang, which scientists think occurred between ten and twenty billion years ago.

Left: A black hole is formed when the mass of a star contracts so compactly that its extremely dense mass has incredibly strong gravity. In theory, a black star will suck in anything that comes within its gravity field, and that object will never be seen again. Even light cannot escape from a black hole. Above: This is the actual size of a black hole of the same mass as the earth. If you were 3600 miles away from it, you would feel a gravitational force similar to the earth's. But if you were two feet away, the force would be 100 million million times stronger.

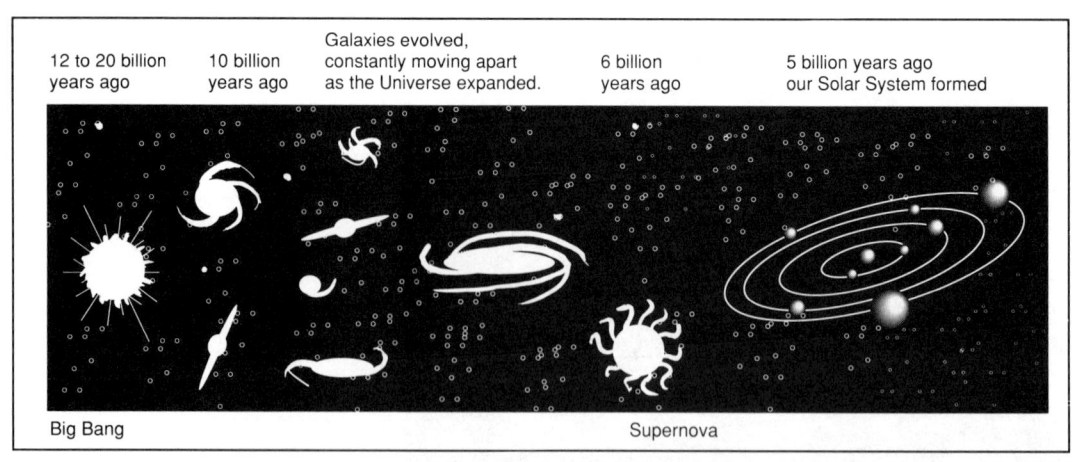

| 12 to 20 billion years ago | 10 billion years ago | Galaxies evolved, constantly moving apart as the Universe expanded. | 6 billion years ago | 5 billion years ago our Solar System formed |

Big Bang — Supernova

This picture shows approximately when scientists believe various cosmic events happened after the Big Bang.

The idea of a big bang was developed and expanded in 1927, not by theoretical physicists, but by a Belgian priest and mathematician named George Lemaitre. He reasoned that if the universe was expanding, it must have been closer together at an earlier time. Lemaitre thought the universe may have begun as "an infinitely small pinpoint...at time 0, 'a day without a yesterday,'" as Timothy Ferris quotes him in *Coming of Age in the Milky Way*. Lemaitre called the pinpoint a "primordial atom" and the explosion a "big noise." British astronomer Arthur S. Eddington disliked Lemaitre's idea. He preferred a more gradual beginning, perhaps with a galaxy. He wrote, "It has seemed to me that the most satisfactory theory would be one which made the beginning not too unaesthetically [not beautiful] abrupt." Scientists have since concluded that Lemaitre had the better idea.

Scientists have developed a theoretical model of the beginning of the physical universe starting one hundredth of a second after the big bang. In *The Cosmic Code*, Heinz Pagels describes the model. At one hundredth of a second, the temperature was one hundred billion degrees Kelvin. (The Kelvin scale uses the same kind of measurement as the Celsius scale, but 0 degrees Kelvin is -273 °C.) The mass was a hot soup made up of electrons, positrons (electron antimatter), neutrinos (which are tiny, massless neutrons), and antineutrinos. In addition, there were a few protons and neutrons, the specks that much later developed into stars and galaxies and, eventually, the earth. But most of the hot soup was exploding matter and antimatter.

At one tenth of a second, the universe had cooled to about ten billion degrees Kelvin. At fourteen seconds, the temperature was one billion degrees Kelvin and the particles and their antiparticles had exploded and disappeared, leaving only electrons, neutrinos, and photons. At three minutes, the mass was settled down enough to combine the original protons and neutrons into nuclei of two kinds, heavy hydrogen (hydrogen with one proton and one neutron) and helium. At one hundred thousand years, atoms formed, and they began the process of forming stars and galaxies. At a few billion years, the universe looked much like what we see today. At some point between five and fifteen billion years, our sun formed.

This model for the beginning leaves questions unanswered. Where did the "primordial atom" come from? Why was it so hot that it exploded? Why did the universe expand into the universe we see today and not some other order? Scientists have begun to speculate on these questions.

In the meantime, scientists use information from two discoveries as evidence that the big bang occurred. The first discovery is Hubble's red shift pattern indicating that the universe is expanding. The second discovery indicates that the universe is cooling according to the curve Max Planck established in the blackbody experiment.

The End of the Universe

Most scientists accept the big bang model for the origin of the universe. And they agree that it will end naturally at some point billions of years in the future. But they do not agree on how that will happen. They speculate about two possible endings—a big crunch or cold silence. The alternatives correspond to the ideas of a closed or an open universe discussed in chapter 3.

A big crunch would happen this way. The outer galaxies would eventually cool to zero as the stars' fuel burns up; then the galaxies would slow down and eventually stop. Gravitational force from the burned out stars would cause them to contract, and the universe

"It seems probable to me that God in the beginning formed matter in solid, massy, hard, unpenetrable, movable particles."

Sir Isaac Newton

"The universe was created from an explosion—it did not exist for all time."

Heinz Pagels, *The Cosmic Code*

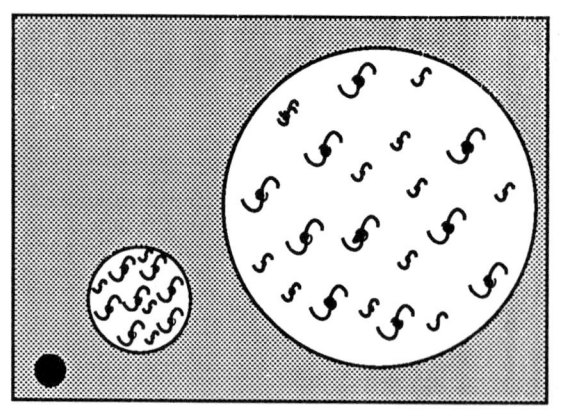

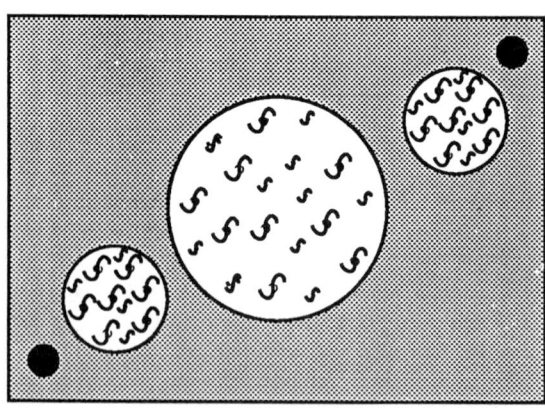

Two theories about the course of the universe are that it is constantly expanding (left), in which case it will end in a quiet whimper, and that it expands and contracts in a continuing cycle (right), in which case it will end in a bang and start all over again.

would backtrack its steps from the big bang. As the mass became smaller and hotter and denser, it would ultimately collapse like a black hole, and the universe would return to a singularity with the mass crunching together infinitely into a "primordial atom." The "primordial atom" could then await the probability of another big bang. The universe could go on infinitely expanding and contracting in very long term cycles.

The cold silent end is a different model. Galaxies would expand infinitely because a gravitational field would be too weak to cause the objects in space to contract and reverse their direction. Either the universe would have too little matter to make a strong enough gravitational field or the gravitational field would have become too weak because the distances between stars would have become too great. Either way, galaxies would keep drifting outward. All the stars would burn up their fuel, collapse, and cool into black dwarfs, or they would become black holes. As the last star goes out, the universe ends in cold, dark silence.

Theories about the end of the universe are even more speculative than the big bang theory about the beginning. The ideas, however, are interesting both to scientists and to nonscientists. Speculation about the beginning and the end of the universe was a popular topic early in the twentieth century, right after World War I and after the publication of Einstein's General Relativity. Two poets reflect the attention paid to the end of the universe.

American poet Robert Frost wrote "Fire and Ice"

around 1919. He wrote,

> Some say the world will end in fire,
> Some say in ice.
> From what I've tasted of desire
> I hold with those who favor fire.

In the late 1920s, T.S. Eliot, another poet, wrote "The Hollow Men," a poem that creates images of a cold, silent end. The poem contains these images: "shape without form," "shade without color," "paralyzed force," "valley of the dying stars," "More distant and more solemn / Than a fading star," "death's twilight kingdom," and "the Shadow." The poem ends with this suggestion of a familiar nursery rhyme:

> *This is the way the world ends*
> *This is the way the world ends*
> *This is the way the world ends*
> *Not with a bang but a whimper.*

The Challenge of Explaining

This book began with priests and ends with poets. In it also are the voices of storytellers and philosophers and scientists. Who best can understand the universe and articulate its order and design? Stephen Hawking, whose mind has been called the most powerful since Einstein's, is working on a unified theory, one that explains the whole universe, including its smallest bit and its greatest distance, its beginning as well as its end. When he commented on the significance of a unified theory at the close of his book, *A Brief History of Time*, this brilliant scientist spoke like a priest or a poet or a philosopher. He said,

> Even if there is only one possible unified theory, it is just a set of rules and equations. What is it that breathes fire into the equations and makes a universe for them to describe?...Why does the universe go to all the bother of existing?...Up to now, most scientists have been too occupied with development of new theories that describe *what* the universe is to ask the question *why*. However, if we do discover a complete theory, it should in time be understandable in broad principle by everyone, not just a few scientists. Then we shall all, philosophers, scientists, and just ordinary people, be able to take part in the discussion of why it is that we and the universe exist.

Scientist Stephen Hawking believes that eventually scientists will discover a unified theory of the universe that will explain in an understandable way what the design of the universe is.

Six

The Search Goes On

Opposite: Theodore Gaster says the mystery of the universe has three threads—magic, religion, and science. Woven together, they may someday tell us what we want to know about the mysteries of the universe.

The desire for order and the designs that explain the universe's mysteries have woven a complex web over thousands of years. In *The New Golden Bough*, Theodore Gaster likened the mystery to a web woven in three threads—"the black thread of magic, the red thread of religion, and the white thread of science." The threads overlap, the web folds back on itself, and it changes from one frame of reference to another, like M and M^1.

Will scientists ever discover a unified theory, one that explains the whole universe? If they do, that theory may in one sense end the mystery of relativity, because all things will be relative to and dependent on all other things. Perhaps scholars may discover that the mystery of relativity is really the mystery of the human mind at work. Perhaps the mystery of the universe exists not so much in nature as it does in human thought. But, for now, the universe is still a mystery, in nature and in the mind.

As the twentieth century draws to a close, we know with certainty much more than we knew at the beginning of the century about the way the universe works and what its limits are. Though our information is more abundant and more accurate, do we live with greater security and wisdom than the primitive person

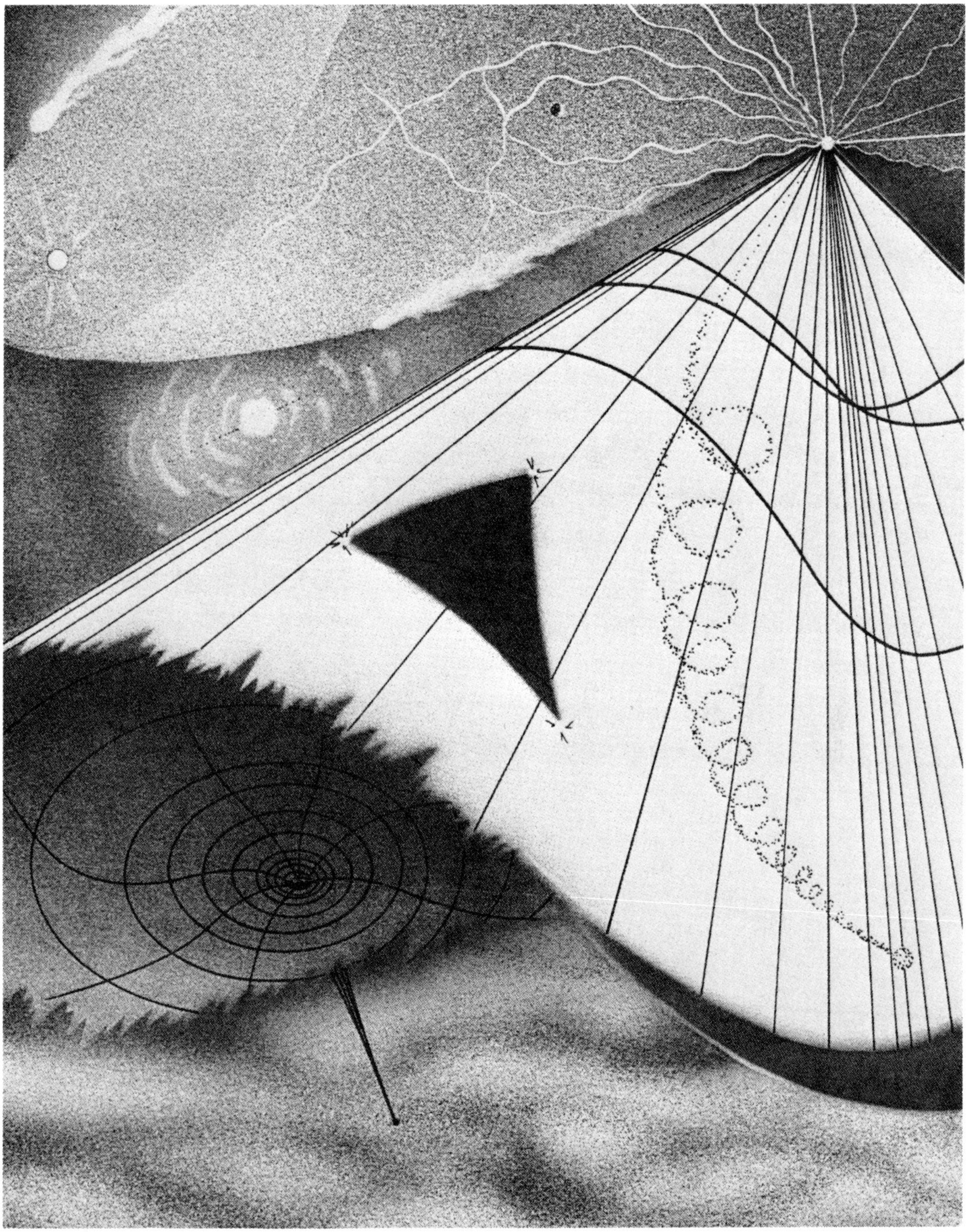

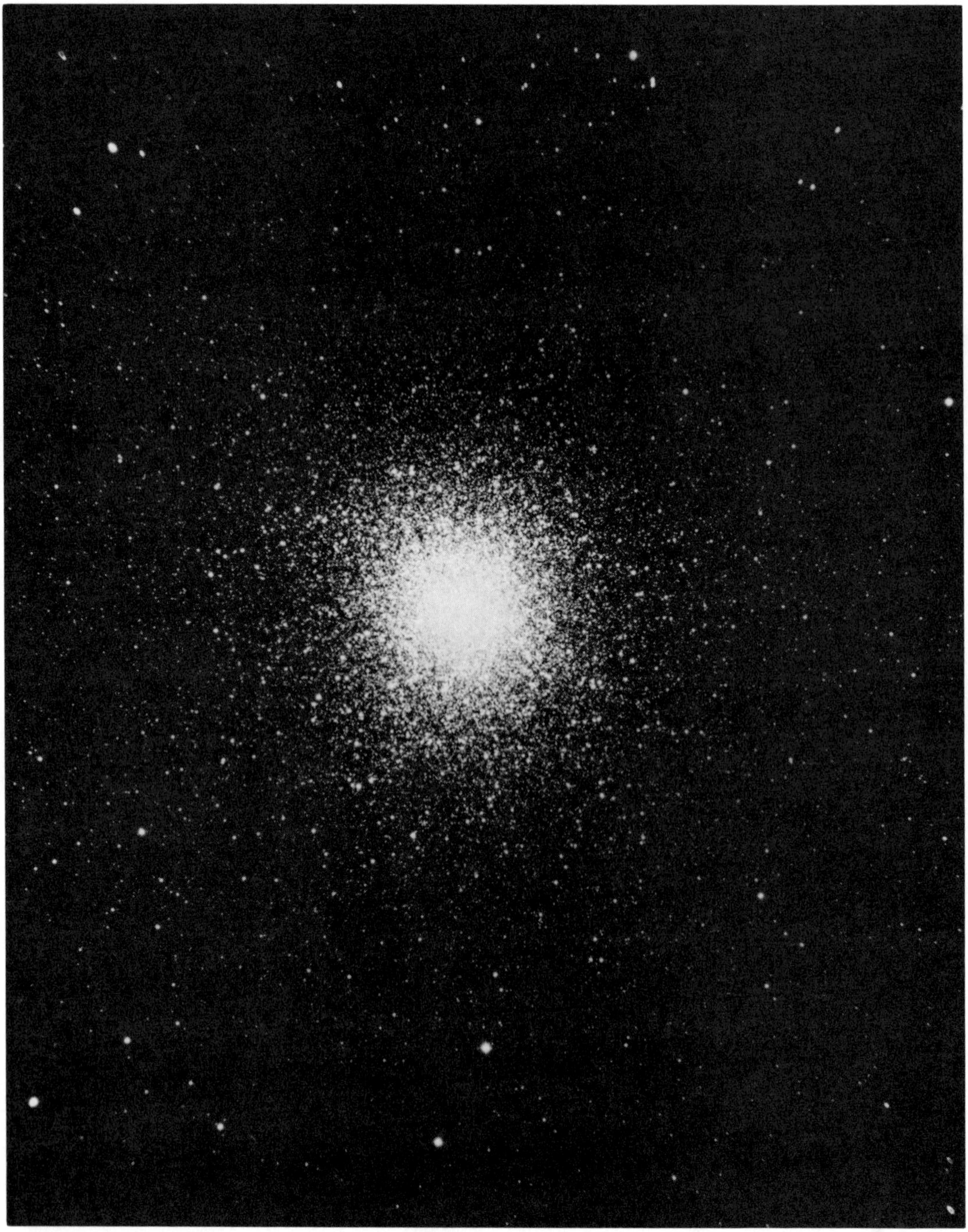

who stuck pins in a doll?

In 1981, scientist and essayist Lewis Thomas said, "The greatest of all accomplishments of twentieth-century science has been the discovery of human ignorance." It is our ignorance that "breathes fire into the equations" and drives us to know "why it is that we and the universe exist." Fortunate it is for human beings that we have minds that want to know. And fortunate it is for our minds that the universe provides us with mysteries to solve. "The advance of knowledge is an infinite progression toward a goal that forever recedes," Theodore Gaster wrote. The mystery goes on.

Opposite: Lewis Thomas said it is human ignorance that "breathes fire into the [scientists'] equations" and drives us to try to discover "why it is that we and the universe exist."

Books for Further Exploration

Irving Adler, *The Wonders of Physics*. New York: Golden Press, 1966.

Necia H. Apfel, *It's All Relative: Einstein's Theory of Relativity*. New York: Lothrop, Lee, & Shepherd, 1981.

David Bergamini, *et al., The Universe*. New York: Time-Life Books, 1962.

William Bixby, *The Universe of Galileo and Newton*. New York: American Heritage Publishing Co., 1964.

Franklyn M. Branley, *The Mystery of Stonehenge*. New York: Thomas Y. Crowell Company, 1969.

J. Bronowski and Milicent E. Selsam, *Biography of an Atom*. New York: Harper and Row, Publishers, 1963.

Eric Chaisson, *Relatively Speaking: Relativity, Black Holes, and the Fate of the Universe*. New York: W. W. Norton & Company, 1988.

Jacqueline Dineen, *Nuclear Power*. Hillside, NJ: Enslow Publishers, Inc., 1986.

Alexander Eliot, *Myths*. New York: McGraw-Hill Book Company, 1976.

Aylesa Forsee, *Albert Einstein: Theoretical Physicist*. New York: The Macmillan Company, 1963.

Herbert Friedman, *The Amazing Universe.* Washington, D.C.: National Geographic Society, 1975.

Roy A. Gallant, *Exploring the Universe.* Garden City, NY: Garden City Books, 1956.

George Gamow, *Thirty Years That Shook Physics: The Story of Quantum Theory.* New York: Doubleday & Company, Inc., 1966.

Virginia Hamilton, *In the Beginning: Creation Stories from Around the World.* New York: Harcourt Brace Jovanovich, 1988.

Charles Hatcher, *The Atom.* London: Macmillan & Co. Ltd., 1963.

Homer, *The Odyssey of Homer.* New York: Oxford University Press, 1932.

Bernard F. Huppe, *Beowulf: A New Translation.* Binghamton, NY: Medieval & Renaissance Texts & Studies, 1987.

D. C. Ipsen, *Isaac Newton: Reluctant Genius.* Hillside, NJ: Enslow Publishers, Inc., 1985.

Herbert Kondo, *Adventures in Space and Time: The Story of Relativity.* New York: Holiday House, 1966.

Arthur C. Lehmann and James E. Myers, *Magic, Witchcraft, and Religion: An Anthropological Study of the Supernatural.* Palo Alto, CA: Mayfield Publishing Company, 1985.

Patrick Moore, *The Picture History of Astronomy.* New York: Grosset and Dunlap, 1972.

Barry Parker, *Einstein's Dream: The Search for a Unified Theory of the Universe.* New York: Plenum Press, 1987.

Rudy Rucker, *The Fourth Dimension.* Boston: Houghton Mifflin Company, 1984.

Harry L. Shipman, *Black Holes, Quasars, and the Universe.* Boston: Houghton Mifflin Company, 1980.

Steven Weinberg, *The First Three Minutes: A Modern View of the Origin of the Universe.* New York: Basic Books, Inc., Publishers, 1977.

Additional Sources Consulted

Fritjof Capra, *The Tao of Physics: An Exploration of the Parallels Between Modern Physics and Eastern Mysticism.* Berkeley, CA: Shambhala Publications, Inc., 1975.

Fritjof Capra, *The Turning Point: Science, Society, and The Rising Culture.* 1982. New York: Bantam Books, 1983.

Albert Einstein, *The Meaning of Relativity.* 1922. Princeton, NJ: Princeton University Press, 1955.

Albert Einstein, *Relativity: The Special and the General Theory.* Trans. Robert W. Lawson. New York: Crown Publishers, Inc., 1961.

Timothy Ferris, *Coming of Age in the Milky Way.* New York: William Morrow and Company, Inc., 1988.

Betty Sue Flowers, ed., *The Power of Myth: Joseph Campbell with Bill Moyers.* New York: Doubleday, 1988.

Roy A. Gallant, *National Geographic Picture Atlas of Our Universe.* Washington, D.C.: National Geographic Society, 1980.

Theodore H. Gaster, ed. *The New Golden Bough* by Sir James George Frazer. New York: Doubleday & Company, Inc., 1961.

Maurice Goldsmith, Alan Mackay, and James Woundhuysen, eds. *Einstein: The First Hundred*

Years. New York: Pergamon Press, 1980.

Stephen W. Hawking, *A Brief History of Time: From the Big Bang to Black Holes.* New York: Bantam Books, 1988.

Paul G. Hewitt, *Conceptual Physics,* 5th ed. Boston: Little, Brown and Company, 1985.

Gerald Holton, *The Advancement of Science, and Its Burdens.* New York: Cambridge University Press, 1986.

Herbert Kondo, *Albert Einstein and the Theory of Relativity.* New York: Franklin Watts, Inc., 1969.

Heinz R. Pagels, *The Cosmic Code: Quantum Physics as the Language of Nature.* New York: Simon and Schuster, 1982.

Edwin E. Slosson, *Easy Lessons in Einstein: A Discussion of the More Intelligible Features of the Theory of Relativity.* New York: Harcourt, Brace and Company, 1920.

Spencer R. Weart and Melba Phillips, eds. *History of Physics.* New York: American Institute of Physics, 1985.

Glossary

Aboriginal — adj. of the earliest known tribe or people in an area.
Absolute — adj. describes any thing or idea that is fixed, certain, in complete and known units.
Accelerator — n. a machine that speeds atomic particles to near the speed of light and then collides them.
Aether — n. a clear, jell-like substance thought at one time to occupy space.
Alpha ray — n. a stream of helium nuclei.
Anthropologist — n. one who studies the cultural habits and behavior of a group of people.
Antimatter — n. all atomic particles with a charge opposite of the original particle's charge, e.g., a proton has a (+); an antiproton a (−).
Astronomer — n. one who studies the stars.
Astrophysics — n. the study combining astronomy and physics.
Atomic number — n. the number of protons and the equal number of electrons in an atom.
Big bang theory — n. the theory that the universe began with a gigantic explosion at a point in time.
Black dwarf — n. a dead star that no longer burns or glows.
Black hole — n. the collapsed remains of a dead massive star with a gravitational force so strong no light is emitted.
Bosons — n. a category of subatomic particles; the force particles in an atom.
Botanist — n. one who studies plants.
Calculate — v. to figure or compute by mathematical methods.
Canopy — n. a covering supported by poles.
Charge — n. a quantity of electric energy identified as positive (+) or negative (−).
Cobbler — n. one who mends shoes.
Collider — n. a machine to speed atomic particles in opposite directions and then smash them into each other.
Complementary — n. Niels Bohr's theory that both wave and particle measurements are needed to make a complete picture of an atomic particle.
Contagion — n. the law of magic stating that once two things have been in contact, they continue to affect each other.
Continuum — n. a continuous series blending into a line or whole.
Converge — n. to come together, meet.
Convert — v. to change into another form.
Curvilinear — adj. formed or characterized by curved lines.
Descendents — n. those relatives that come after; later generations.
Determinism — n. the doctrine that all facts and events exemplify nature's laws, that all events have causes.
Discrete — adj. detached from others, separate, distinct, opposite of a continuum.
Diverge — v. to move apart, to separate.
Eclipse — n. the lining up of sun, earth, and moon so that one comes between and casts a shadow. In a lunar eclipse, the earth goes between the sun and moon and blocks out the sunlight shining on the moon.
Electromagnetism — n. the phenomena that says electric energy and magnetism are equivalent.
Electron — n. the orbiting particle in an atom with a negative charge.
Elements — n. the class of substances that make up all matter.
Elliptical — adj. in the shape of a slightly-flattened circle.
Embankment — n. a bank or mound built along a road or railroad tracks.
Empirical — adj. derived from observation and experience, verifiable by experiment.
Euclidean geometry — n. a mathematics originated by Euclid to measure flat space.
Event — n. a happening in a particular place at a specific time.
Fantasies — n. mental images originating in the imagination.
Fermions — n. category of subatomic particles composed of the matter particles.
Fission — n. the process of separating an atom into two new atoms.
Frame of reference — n. a place or position from which an event is seen.
Fusion — n. the process of combining two light

atoms into a different, heavier atom.
Gaming house — n. a gambling place.
Geometry — n. the branch of mathematics that deals with measuring space.
Homeopathic — adj. a kind of magic that assumes that like produces like, the Law of Similarity.
Hyperbola — n. a geometric shape, opposite of a sphere.
Imply — v. to suggest without stating directly.
Indivisible — adj. not able to be divided.
Inertia, inertial — n. adj. the property of matter in which it remains at rest or travels in a straight line unless acted on.
Inexplicable — adj. not able to be explained.
Innumerable — adj. so many it is not possible to count them all.
Intuitive — adj. the mental process whereby an idea comes to mind all at once whole.
Invariant — n. a quantity or expression that is constant throughout a range of conditions.
Kelvin scale — n. a scale to measure temperature. On a Kelvin scale 0 is equal to -460° on the Fahrenheit scale.
Light year — n. the distance light travels in a year at 186,000 miles per second, about six trillion miles.
Lookback time — n. seeing an object in space as it appeared in the past, according to the number of light years it takes for its light to reach earth.
Mass — n. the amount of matter in a body, measured by the amount of energy it takes to start or stop it.
Matrix — n. the rectangular arrangement of numbers in columns and rows.
Matter — n. the physical substance of a solid, liquid, or gas.
Neutrino — n. a small massless neutron.
Neutron — n. the particle in the atom's nucleus that has no electric charge.
Nuclear physics — n. the branch of physics concerned with the study of subatomic parts, primarily the atom's nucleus.
Nucleus — n. the matter core of an atom, made up of protons and neutrons.
Objective, objectivity — adj., n. an action or a perception not affected by human feeling or action.
Observatory — n. a place set up for viewing stars.
Particle detector — n. a device to identify and measure particles smashed in an accelerator or a collider.
Philosophy — n. the study of ideas and principles based on reason.
Photon — n. a quanta of light.
Postulate — n. a claim or rule or assumption in a theory.
Predictable — adj. able to determine the outcome ahead of time.
Prehistoric — adj. describing events that occur before recorded history.
Probability — n. the frequency with which an event occurs or is likely to occur.
Proton — n. the positively-charged particle in an atom's nucleus.
Psychological — adj. pertaining to a person's mind, feelings or motivation.
Quadrant — n. an instrument with graduated measurements for measuring altitudes.
Quantum, quanta — n. the singular and plural for quantity or amount.
Quark — n. an elementary particle thought to be the smallest building block in the universe.
Quasar — n. the stars at the farthest measured distance thought to be forming into young galaxies.
Radiate, radiation — v., n. to transfer energy by means of electromagnetic waves or high-speed particles.
Random — adj. occurring according to no pattern or order, unpredictable.
Red giant — n. a massive star burning its last fuel before it goes out.
Relative — adj. in connection to or comparison with some other thing.
Relativity — n. the theory of measuring one thing in connection with another.
Repel — v. to push away. Like charges repel.
Renaissance — n. means rebirth. The name of an era when learning flourished.
Revelation — n. knowledge suddenly disclosed or revealed.
Satellite — n. a body, a moon, that revolves around a planet.
Shells — n. the layers of orbiting spaces in which electrons orbit around the nucleus in an atom.
Similarity — n. a law of magic which states that like produces like.
Singularity — n. a point in time at which gravitational force curves space infinitely and time stops.
Sirens — n. mythical sea nymphs, part woman

and part bird, whose singing is very beautiful.
Solstice — n. either of two times during the year when the sun is the greatest distance from the equator, causing the greatest difference between the length of day and night: about June 21 and December 22.
Spectroscope — n. an instrument that indicates colors by lines, used to determine whether a star is moving toward or away from the earth.
Sphere — n. a round body.
Spin — n. the momentum of an elementary particle, the number of times it turns before it returns to the original.
Supernatural power — n. a being with power above and beyond natural or human power.
Supernova — n. the explosion of a star.
Symbol — n. an object or form that represents something else.
Symmetry — n. balanced proportions; a design that is the same on both sides of a center axis.
Telescope — n. an instrument equipped with powerful lenses used to see stars.
Theory — n. a model of the universe or part of it with rules for proving or testing the model.
Transformation theory — n. Paul Dirac's theory that shows how to arrive at a single result from wave mechanics and matrix mechanics.
Tunneling — v. the appearance of a particle in its least likely place, as if it moved through a wall.
Uncertainty principle — n. the amount of inaccuracy one finds when trying to measure a particle.
Uniform — adj. the steady pace and continuous direction of an object in special relativity.
Uranium — n. a heavy atom, one with 235 combined protons and neutrons and one with 238.
Velocity — n. the speed and direction of a body.
Wavelength — n. the distance from crests through trough to next crest of a wave.
White dwarf — n. a star that has burned all its fuel and shrunk, but is still hot.

Index

Anderson, Carl, 97
Aristarchus, 37-38
Aristotle, 28, 30-31, 32-33, 36, 41, 50, 72
astronomy, 38-39, 42, 44, 109
  and physics, 92-94
  and relativity, 65-67
  in history, 27-32, 35, 36, 39-41
atom, 72, 74-75, 77, 78-79, 80-83, 85-86, 88-89
  discovery of, 33, 72
  experiments with, 96-99
  physics of, 60, 94-96, 101-102
    ethics of, 102
  see also matter

Bacon, Francis, 36, 37
Bohr, Niels, 81, 82-83, 87
Born, Max, 79, 84-85
Bose, Satyendra Nath, 100
Brahe, Tycho, 36, 38, 39
de Broglie, Louis, 84, 87
Brown, Robert, 77
Bunsen, Robert, 103

Capra, Fritjof, 97, 104
Copernicus, Nicolaus, 30, 36, 37-38, 42

Democritus, 33, 72
Descartes, René, 36, 37
Dirac, Paul, 87, 88, 89, 97, 100
Doppler, Christian Johann, 103-104

Eddington, Arthur S., 110
Einstein, Albert
  life of, 33, 46, 48-49, 50-51
  theories of
    general relativity, 48, 61-67
    quantum physics, 71, 75-76, 77-78, 89
    special relativity, 48, 51-58, 61
Empedocles, 33
energy
  in relativity, 56-58, 59, 60-61
Euclid, 33, 66
Eudoxus, 28, 30

Faraday, Michael, 49, 50
Fermi, Enrico, 100-101
Ferris, Timothy, 35, 74, 85, 101, 106, 110
fission, 94-95
fusion, 94, 95-96

Galilei, Galileo, 32, 36, 39-42, 105
Gaster, Theodore H., 65, 85, 114, 115
Gell-Mann, Murray, 101
gravity, 31, 35, 41, 42, 43-45, 62, 63-66, 67, 70

Hale, George Ellery, 103
Hawking, Stephen, 10, 99, 101, 106, 108, 113
Heisenberg, Werner, 81, 87, 88
Holt, Gerald, 102
Hubble, Edwin, 104

Kepler, Johannes, 36, 38-39
Kirchhoff, Gustav, 103

Lederman, Leon, 102
Lemaitre, George, 110
light
  definition of, 33
  in black holes, 108
  in relativity, 51, 61, 62-63, 65, 75, 76-77
  experiments with, 50, 69
  speed of, 54, 58, 60

magic
  law of contagion, 14, 15
  law of similarity, 13-14
  primitive, 14, 15, 17, 23, 36-37
magnetism, 49-50, 62
matter
  and antimatter, 94, 97-99, 111
  definition of, 33, 57-59
  particles of, 97, 99, 101, 110-111
Maxwell, James Clerk, 49, 50
Medewar, Sir Peter, 102
Michelson, Albert, 49, 50
Morley, Edward, 50

nature
  definition of, 11-12
Newton, Sir Isaac, 36, 42-45, 46, 48, 55, 101, 111

Pagels, Heinz, 61, 65, 78, 79, 85, 88, 89, 91, 94, 110, 111
Pauli, Wolfgang, 83
physics
  Einsteinian, 51-71
  Newtonian, 42-45, 46, 55
Planck, Max, 55, 75, 76, 88, 111
Plato, 28-30, 33, 36

Ptolemy, 28, 31-32, 36
Pythagoras, 33

quantum theory, 71, 76, 77, 82, 85-86, 87-89, 91, 92

relativity
   early theories, 24, 28-33
   Einstein's theories of, 24, 46-71, 92
   in the Bible, 21
Rutherford, Ernest, 76, 78-79, 81

Schrödinger, Erwin, 87, 88
solar system
   age of, 34, 96
   in the galaxy, 105
   view of
     as earth-centered, 11, 26, 27-32, 34
     as sun-centered, 11, 35, 37-39, 41-42
speed
   definition of, 51-54
   in relativity, 59, 60, 65
   of light, 104-105
stars, 106-109
Stonehenge, 26-27

telescope, 40
Thomas, Lewis, 115

time
   in space, 105, 108
   definition of, 21, 32-33, 34
     by relativity, 51-52, 53-54, 55, 64-65
   early measurement of, 26-27

universe
   definition of, 11, 30, 32
   forces of, 61-62, 101, 105
   life of
     future
       as continually expanding, 67, 69, 104-105, 109, 112
       as eventually shrinking, 67-69, 111-112
       poetry about, 112-113
     origin
       as gradual, 110
       in the big bang, 108-111
     stars in, 106-109
   Newtonian theory of, 45, 46, 79
   relativity theory of, 32, 61-66, 71, 91
   study of, 103-104
   unified theory of, 113, 114
   views of,
     biblical, 19-22, 34
     in heroic epic, 17-19
     historic, 27-32, 34, 35
     prehistoric, 11, 13-14, 17, 24-26

Acknowledgements

When I undertook the task of writing a book about relativity, I wanted to make a point. I wanted to show that Einstein's Theory of Relativity and quantum mechanics are not such incomprehensible theories that there is no point in trying to understand them. I once thought they were, and I know many people who feel the ideas are beyond their grasp. I now believe they are at least partially understandable to a wide audience. I decided to put them in a philosophical and historical context and to connect them to familiar experiences whenever possible. This is what I tried to do; readers will have to decide whether I accomplished my goal.

I have had generous help from many people; I especially want to thank a few of them. I want to thank George Drier, chairperson of the science department at the school where I teach; he read the manuscript to check facts and principles of physics. I want to thank Karin Swisher, the first reader, who helped me keep the sentences clear and the topics in balance. The editor, Terry O'Neill, suggested many improvements. She sent me pages of comments and enough markings to make the first draft look like a roadmap. Her direction helped me to give the book better form, and I am grateful to her. Finally, I want to thank Barbara Preston, who followed the revisions and prepared the manuscript.

Picture Credits

Hansen Planetarium, 9
Cabisco Teleproductions, copyright 1989 Carolina Biological Supply Company, 10, 113
Palomar Observatory photograph, 12L, 108, 116
Stock, Boston: James R. Holland 12C; Cary Wolinsky 12R; Clif Gorboden 13T; Elizabeth Crews 13B; Michael Hayman 15T; Joseph Schuyler 16; Anna Kaufman Moon 22; Jerry Howard 26T; Dean Abramson 53R; Michael Weisbrot 54; Michael Grecco 57; Frank Siteman 80L, 86L; Peter Menzel 103; Ellis Herwig 104
The Bettmann Archive, 14, 15B, 18, 19, 20, 25, 28, 29, 34B, 35, 36T, 38, 39L, 40, 41, 43, 56L, 56R, 90
C. M. Dixon, 26B
Ptolemy, *The Almagest*, 31
Courtesy Burndy Library, Norwalk, CT, 33, 36B, 37R, 39R, 50T, 50B, 76, 105T
Mary Ahrndt, 34T, 44, 52, 62, 66, 75, 77, 78R, 82, 83B, 86R, 95, 96, 109L, 110, 112
Photo by Owen Gingerich, 37L
Courtesy of the Archives, California Institute of Technology, 47
Annalen der Physik (1905), 51
© Magnum/Erich Lessing, 53L, 55, 58B, 67L, 70, 73
Steve Berg, 58T, 60
Stanford Linear Accelerator Center and U.S. Department of Energy, 61
By permission of the Hebrew University of Jerusalem, Israel, 49, 63, 71
A.I.P. Niels Bohr Library, 67R, 78L (photo by C. Wynn-Williams), 81 (Weisskopf Collection, photo by P. Ehrenfest, Jr.), 83T & 87T (Francis Simon Collection), 105B (Hale Observatories)
Heinz Pagels, *The Cosmic Code*, copyright © 1982 by Heinz R. Pagels; reprinted by permission of Simon & Schuster, Inc., 64, 68, 69, 80R, 84
From *Conceptual Physics*, 5th edition, by Paul G. Hewitt; copyright © 1985 by Paul G. Hewitt; reprinted by permission of HarperCollins Publishers, 87B, 88
Mount Wilson and the Las Campanas Observatories, Carnegie Institution of Washington, 93
Fermilab, Visual Media Services, 97, 98
Reprinted from *A Brief History of Time* by Stephen Hawking; Bantam, Doubleday, Group Publishing Inc., © 1988 Stephen Hawking, art copyright © Ron Miller, 100
National Archives, 102
Reproduced from *Relatively Speaking* by Eric Chaisson, illustrated by Lola Judith Chaisson, with the permission of W. W. Norton and Company, Inc.; © 1988 by Eric J. Chaisson; drawings © 1988 by Lola Judith Chaisson, 107, 115.
Reprinted from *The Key to the Universe* by Nigel Calder, copyright © 1977 Nigel Calder, Viking Press, NY, 109R

About the Author

Clarice Swisher lives in St. Paul, Minnesota. A teacher of literature, from time to time she has told her students, "Pay attention to the physicists; their ideas show up in the literature." Writing this book has confirmed her belief that scientists and poets begin with the same essential questions, and sometimes their searches for order cross paths.